Book 2 in the Freedom's Fire Series

A novel by

Bobby Adair

Website: www.bobbyadair.com

Twitter: www.twitter.com/BobbyAdairBooks

Facebook: www.facebook.com/BobbyAdairAuthor

Mailing list for new book alerts:

www.bobbyadair.com/subscribe

Report typos:

www.bobbyadair.com/typos

COVER DESIGN

Alex Saskalidis, a.k.a. 187designz

COVER ILLUSTRATION

Illustration © Tom Edwards
TomEdwardsDesign.com

EDITING & BOOK FORMATTING

Kat Kramer Adair

SPECIAL THANKS

Mike & Re Kramer

Aaron Landau and the folks at
EVO3 Workspace in Frisco, Colorado

Chapter 1

Who risks death when a half-assed lie is enough to guarantee life?

Pretty much nobody.

Orange-suited SDF troopers are cycling out through the warehouse's airlock, stepping into the bleak vacuum over the asteroid's surface, empty-handed and angry-eyed.

Is it the loss of their ships and the death of their comrades that's left them bitter? Is it their short imprisonment?

Or is it the charade they play?

How many of these mutineers are liars who were afraid to lose their lives when others in their platoons chose rebellion? Did they each raise a hand and say 'Me too' for fear of being executed and ejected into space? How many made that choice in hopes of finding a chance to get away later?

With each burp of the airlock, more empty helmets go in, and more SDF mutineers come out.

Blair is trying to organize them into their platoons without much help. We're short on officers, and the sergeants are showing the inexperience of their fresh stripes and simulator training. None has seen as much war as Brice.

The only organizing most of the sergeants have engaged in was lining their squads up for orderly loading into the grav lifts back at the Silverthorne spaceport. The only leading they did was through the chaos of the bombardment in Arizona, herding their troops into the assault ships. "Run that way and get on that ship or die!" Probably the only order most of these sergeants has ever barked.

My god, the non-coms are little better than hall monitors.

Blair directs the loitering troops to scavenge weapons from the dead Trogs. She's taking charge, and is obviously comfortable with it. Everybody seems perfectly satisfied to act on her commands. She's now a colonel—her SDF rank has translated seamlessly into the same rank in our tiny insurgent army.

My major rank did, too.

Do we humans so desperately hunger for structure that we'll accept any, even if the legitimacy is nothing more than a shoulder decoration left over from a previous job?

I guess.

So, I listen for instructions. Why not?

I've already done all I knew to do, or guessed to do on my own, following my steps as one led to another. I brought two of my company's ships to the Free Army's asteroid base. I led a commando-style raid to take out the Trogs defending the surface and manning the anti-ship guns. With the help of my squad, I freed the prisoners, sent Jill and her platoon away in the mining tug to dispose of the damaged Trog cruiser, and directed our only functioning assault ship off the surface in case the battle for the mining colony isn't over.

Now, nothing is happening except organizational bullshit. I'm awaiting instructions, and Blair is in her element, providing them to everyone her eye falls upon.

I'm starting to think maybe my place in the world—my natural element—is in combat. Weird to imagine that for a guy who's spent his whole life constructing an elaborate lie to live behind, while pushing plate after plate after plate down the grav fab line.

My life has been nothing but lies and fantasies.

And a nagging, yet distant danger.

People in charge of the world like to hang spies and rebels who don't appreciate the status quo. That's one thing the siege didn't change.

Still, when the Trogs were swinging their blue disruptor blades and coming to kill me, you know, for being on their ship and trying to destroy it, I was just as frightened as the next grunts in the platoon, yet didn't succumb to it. I didn't think about dying. I didn't dwell on it, anyway.

I just did what needed doing.

Maybe that was luck, one fortunate event on top of another. If I'd cowered, if I'd doubted, or overthought everything trying to find the safest approach, I think I'd be dead right now and so would every man and woman on my ship. Well, if not dead, then consigned to a serf's future, not any different from the past we're all trying to escape.

At the moment though, I'm bored.

I'm staring at the black sky, watching Jill's mining tug slowly shrink to a pinprick of reflected light as it races through space to catch the damaged Trog cruiser and push it so far away that it's ten thousand Trog legionnaires won't be a danger to us.

I wonder, does the boredom make me normal or something else?

Does it matter?

Is it just that some people are cut out for the logistical side of war, and some aren't?

And is it not just that I have an aptitude for fighting, now that I've glimpsed at the clarity of life through the lens of mortal struggle, tasted deathly fear as it courses through my veins and dribbles onto my taste buds, and rode the wave of victorious elation with my enemy's blood on my blade and his body under my boots, I have to ask, am I an addict?

I do crave another helping.

"Are you as surprised as I am?" asks Sergeant Brice.

I turn to see him walking up beside me while ejecting the magazine from his railgun and checking to see how many rounds are left.

"What are we talking about?" I ask.

"That we lived through that."

I shrug. Twenty-four hours ago I was on earth and had never seen a Trog in real life. "I don't have a frame of reference." But in my heart, I think I know. "I take it this isn't a typical day for SDF troopers."

Brice laughs. It's that dark laugh of his, not mean, but twisted black by too many days dodging the reaper's scythe. "Mostly we just die."

"Maybe I'm surprised."

"That we're not dead?"

"I guess," I admit. "Truth is, I was just thinking about that. I want to stay alive as much as the next guy. I just don't expect I'll be the one who catches a bullet or who's cleaved by a Trog. Maybe that's conceit, or it might be delusion." I shrug. "I don't care which."

"You shouldn't," says Brice. "You don't want to question things too much. Questions turn to doubts, and doubts undermine a soldier's confidence. Call it conceit. Call it whatever, but sometimes, it's all you've got."

"Maybe all you need?" I ask.

"All you needed when you told us we were ramming those Trog cruisers," confirms Brice. "All you needed when you stormed that bridge all by yourself."

I laugh. "That wasn't the plan, exactly."

"Just turned out that way?" Brice chuckles.

"And maybe imagination," I add. "Maybe it's the intangible mix of both. You think of something crazy, and then believe you're indestructible enough to pull it off. Maybe that surprised the Trogs as much as anything."

Nodding, Brice concludes and affirms, "They're dead. We're not."

"They never imagined a handful of humans could attack them like we did," I say. "So of course they never expected it, never dreamed to look for it, and that was a huge part of our success. It's easier to shoot a Trog not shooting back because he's busy eating his lunch and not imagining you're behind him."

"So that's it, Napoleon?" Brice laughs, "Surprise, conceit, and imagination, the ingredients of victory?"

I don't say anything. I'm not sure if Brice is laughing at me or if he's giddy on a post-battle high. Instead, I start thinking about the cost of the victory. Half of my squad died, half of my platoon is gone. Half of my company was blown to bits while their ships were rocketing into space from the Arizona shipyard. They never even tasted war.

In total, the company is nearing seventy-percent casualties in the first twenty-four hours.

Holy Christ!

"What's the matter," Brice asks. "Your face just changed." He looks me up and down. "Your catheter slip out? You got shit dripping down your leg?"

"Casualties," I tell him.

He stops his train of thought, probably runs a quick estimate on the numbers and morosely says, "Get used to it."

"I don't want to."

"That's admirable," he tells me, as his gaze wanders over to Hastings' body, and it seems suddenly inappropriate that she's still there on the ground, slowly freezing solid.

I look around. Trog dead are scattered everywhere. Some are on the ground. Some are floating, waiting for the asteroid's micro-g to finally pull them down. One body is at knee-height, stiff, but spinning in the vacuum as its suit vents gas through a small hole under the arm. Morbidly hypnotic.

All those Chinese SDF corpses are stacked like firewood along the warehouse's exterior wall. Hundreds of them.

I think about all those Trogs I saw in the hangar of the cruiser we rammed, grasping onto anything to keep from being sucked into space as they slowly suffocated. How many were in there, dying as I watched, dying because I killed them? They seemed like humans—ugly humans—live, thinking beings.

But God, I hate them.

"The thought you need to take to heart," says Brice, punching me in my sternum, "is that we're in the army." He emphasizes the next part. "This is war." He lets that hang on the comm between us for a moment. "It's a shitty war, that we're losing, and that doesn't matter, because you know what? Even if we were winning, people would still die."

I take a half-step back out of fist range.

"I hate to see it when that happens," he says. "I hate it more than you know." Brice stares for a few long, uncomfortable moments into my eyes, drilling me aggressively, rudely, like he's caught me washing my dick in the shower a little too long, like he's looking for things that are none of his business, and he's finding them.

I find something to glance at over the horizon. Anything to turn away from his interrogating eyes.

"You'll know," he tells me. "You have an inkling. I see it in you. It hurts you to lose people." He nods slowly. "It's like they're your kids, almost. You're responsible for them." He steps close, balls his fist, and taps his knuckles roughly against my sternum again. "You feel it here every time one dies. They'll haunt your memories. You'll see their faces when you close your eyes, and you'll hear them scream when you're trying to be alone with your thoughts." He shakes his head as his lips curl up around an unpleasant taste. "You'll never be alone again, never. They'll always be there with you."

He steps away from me, turns, and scans the horizon, collecting his thoughts for another moment before he goes on. "I think you need to feel that to be a good officer, or sergeant, or whatever you are when you're responsible for someone else's life. Just as importantly, you have to be able to trade those lives away when you need to. Maybe that's what makes a good officer, knowing what it costs to swap lives for objectives, but being able to do it just the same."

I start running through numbers in my head again. Three Trog cruisers. No, four now. At least ten thousand Trogs on each, and that's just in the battle legions they keep in the barracks in the back. What, another four or five thousand Trogs and Grays to fly the ship and keep the railgun hoppers full of slugs? Four ships, and sixty thousand Trogs? Holy shit. Sixty thousand. The rough math churns out the result, though I can't say the number with any pride. There's too much weird emotion stuck all over it. In an assault ship with forty troops ready to die—ready to do what I tell them, I'm a Hiroshima bomb. "The objective has to be worth it."

"Damn well better be," says Brice. "And you need to be willing to die right along with them. The objective has to be worth your life, too. Your troops need to see that in you if you want their loyalty."

Sixty fucking thousand?

How goddamn deep is my hate?

Or is that just war?

I fear I'm so far out of my depth that my fake leadership is apparent to everyone who sees me, and my insecurity comes to the surface. "Am I doing that, winning their loyalty? Their respect?"

"Yeah, you are," says Brice, nodding. "I don't know how long any of us in this company are going to live with you in charge. You're dragging us into some crazy shit. We're all behind you, because we're winning. That's better than what we were doing before, dying for nothing."

Chapter 2

"Kane," calls Silva over the comm, "Kane?"

I look up. Silva and Mostyn are up there in the sky with gray asteroid dust clinging to their orange suits. They're hard to make out against the black of space. Lenox, not yet coated with dust, is easier to spot. "What do you have?" I'm looping Brice and Blair into the conversation as I look at my d-pad to see who's on.

"A dozen Trogs are filing out of one of the railgun pits."

She's talking about the railguns we disabled when we first attacked the mining colony. Each had a door down at the bottom, undoubtedly connecting them to a tunnel system.

"Why am I just now hearing about this?" snaps Blair.

"I just looped you in," I tell her, not understanding her anger.

"If we've got Trogs coming," she clucks, "I need to know right away, because I'm in charge. I need to—"

"Chill, bitch," says Silva, cutting her off. "Who are you again?"

"I'm your commanding officer," Blair points out, her voice seething. "If you don't like it, I can kill switch you and your whole platoon."

Kill switch?

"Listen," I nearly shout. "Blair—"

"Colonel Blair," she clarifies.

"Colonel Blair," I acquiesce, "let's talk about all this bullshit after we figure out what the Trog situation is. I looped you in as soon as Silva called with the report."

Brice is looking over at Blair, standing a good twenty meters away, and I can tell by the expression on his face, he's contemplating giving her the Milliken treatment—a railgun round right through the faceplate.

I shake my head, just enough for him to see. If Blair is serious about her kill-switch authority, it may be that she's got all of us tied to her biosensor, so if she dies, every rebel on the asteroid does, too.

Brice understands, and instead of ventilating Blair with a burst of railgun slugs, he says, "Trogs don't do anything with just a hundred or two hundred soldiers." He looks at me to confirm that his subversive thoughts are set aside for later. "I think a thousand Trogs is the basic unit."

"Basic unit?" asks Blair.

"Like a platoon for us," he answers. "We break down to fireteams of two or three, and squads of five to ten, but the platoon is the basic building block of the SDF. When we send troops into battle, they go as a platoon. Forty is the SDF standard."

"So you think there might be eight or nine hundred below the surface?" asks Blair, doing the math. She sounds like she's afraid.

"That's what I'm saying," answers Brice. "One thing you need to understand. For an enemy we've been at war with for two years, we know pitifully little about them. So don't take my word as gospel."

"I've got at least fifty out of that hole," says Silva, "and they're still coming."

"Toward us?" Brice asks.

"Just exiting and loitering," says Silva. "Not coming this way, yet."

"Lenox," I call.

She answers the question I'm going to ask. "I'm already deploying my squad in positions to defend the warehouse."

I'm guessing there are still a hundred prisoners inside.

"That's fine," says Blair, like she was the one Lenox was talking to.

Mostyn says, "Kane, I see them coming out of another gun pit on the other side of the mine. Both emplacements on the far end, the first two we took out."

It crosses my mind that Mostyn is skipping right past Blair to piss her off.

Brice smirks for me to see, points in the direction of the strip mine, then toward the railgun emplacements a kilometer away. "They're massing. There must be a few dozen airlocks in this complex they can exit from—maybe twice that many. They know we're slaughtering them when they attack in small numbers. The Trogs are falling back on a tactic they know works. They're going to gather their force and overwhelm us."

"Is that gospel?" asks Blair, harshly.

Unprofessional, I'm thinking. She needs to learn how to lead, not just lurk in the shadows like an MSS officer, pouncing on mistakes.

"As gospel as it gets," Brice tells her, ignoring her tone.

"We've got some time, then," I announce. "Silva, Mostyn, keep a close watch. Let me know as soon as the Trogs start moving. Lenox, I want you up here near the colony where you can see your squad and keep an eye on surface installations."

"Already here," she answers.

I look up to see her orange suit moving across the sky, headed exactly where I would have put her. I decide she's more than competent. Maybe I'm not the only one born for this shit.

"We need more people up there," says Blair, past her tantrum and back to pragmatic bureaucrat.

Surprised, both Brice and I are stunned by the quick switch in tone.

"Okay," I answer. "Brice, get with the other sergeants who are out of the warehouse and find us three or four more lookouts who have good grav control and can fly in low g."

Blair is walking toward us, giving me a nod like I've done a good job at conveying her orders, and I'm more than a little put off by it. Still talking to Brice, I say, "Make it six for lookouts. And find us a handful of volunteers who can fly. We need to reconstitute our squad."

"Will do." Brice turns and hurries out among the troops who'd been prisoners and still look like a disorganized mob of protesters.

Blair tells me, "I need to approve unit transfers."

"Fine," I'm not at all liking the way this relationship with her is turning out. "What's our status? How many armed soldiers do we have?"

"What's our status, *ma'am*?" she clarifies for me.

My God, back to this shit?

Standing by me now, she looks up at our three lookouts overhead, to remind me they're on the comm line.

I try not to sound like an angry seventh grader when I ask, "What's our status, *Ma'am*?"

"In addition to your platoon," she tells me, "we've moved nearly sixty out. Half of those are armed with single-shot Trog weapons. Most of the others have Trog swords."

"Disruptors." I'd hoped for better. Only the members of my platoon who are still alive are armed with automatic railguns, the only advantage we have over the Trogs so far. "We can't win if we fight them with their weapons."

"I know." She's looking around nervously.

"Any idea where the Trogs stashed the soldiers' guns after they captured the assault ships, Ma'am?"

Blair shakes her head. "I've got Sergeant Billings on it. He's asking around, and he's organizing a squad to search."

"That'll be dangerous, Ma'am."

"We have to have those weapons," she tells me like I don't know it.

"Might I suggest, Ma'am," God this suck-up, military-discipline shit is a pain in the ass, "to make sure Billings and his squad go out armed. That's all I'm saying. They'll have to enter airlocks not knowing what's on the other side—probably Trogs. The only question is how many."

"Or it could be more prisoners," she counters.

"Do we have a map of the underground structure of this base, Ma'am?" I ask. "Anything?"

"Nothing," she tells me. "It's all top secret. All I knew about this place was the location I passed to you back on earth."

I tell Silva, Mostyn, and Lenox, I'm dropping them from the conversation and leave them instructions to keep me updated when things change with our growing Trog infestation.

"What about the miners?" I ask Blair, skipping the *Ma'am* now that it's just us. "What about Free Army personnel? They must have been here before, right? We didn't just plan to show up here and invade, did we?"

"Of course not," she snaps, taking my question as an accusation, just like it was meant. "This is *our* base."

"Was," I correct her.

"*Is,*" she insists. "And we need to take it back. That's our number one priority, the only goal we can afford." She looks around. "What alternative do we have? We have one operational ship, and one tug chasing a crippled Trog cruiser toward Jupiter."

I don't comment on that, though I know she means it as an insult. I ordered Jill Rafferty off in the tug. It was the right decision considering the risk of all those live Trogs still aboard the cruiser.

"None of our assault ships can fly without extensive repairs," she concludes. "We can't leave."

She's 100% right about that. The best we can do is prepare for the coming attack. No, not the best. "Might I suggest we send out a second recon squad, not just Sergeant Billings. It'll be dangerous, but we need to find those automatic weapons. We need to know how many Trogs are on this base. We need to know what the subterranean levels look like. We won't win if we react out of ignorance. If we're going to take this base from however many Trogs are here, we need to be proactive."

CHAPTER 3

Blair takes a moment to tap on her d-pad and double-check that she and I are on a private comm link. She doesn't want any other ears listening in by accident. Standing in front of me now, she looks at me with an impassive face, yet her words come out dripping in acid. "We need to get a few things straight."

I try to keep all inflection out of my voice, while knowing that we're preparing for an attack we're not likely to survive. We need to move this thing, whatever it is, along. "I'm listening."

"I'm a colonel. You're a major. I outrank you. We need to maintain the chain of command."

"Is this about the 'yes, ma'am' thing again, ma'am?" Maybe throwing the ma'am on the end was a bit childish. I'm already irritated with the conversation.

"The troops need to see me in charge. The orders need to pass from me to you, from there to the captains and lieutenants—"

I interrupt. "We don't have any captains, and only a few lieutenants."

"—and from them to the sergeants and enlisted personnel."

"Enlisted?" I ask, slipping into the trap of the argument. "Hardly anyone here is enlisted. These are all draftees. And that doesn't matter anyway, does it? We're all rebels now, right? We're mutineers and murderers. We're volunteers in the Free Army." I wave a dismissive hand at the mining colony on our potato-shaped asteroid. "Free Army? With one shitty base so far from the middle of nowhere that nowhere doesn't even know we're here?" I'm sprinting into rant mode. "You tell me there's more to this fucking fiasco—and by God, I hope so—yet you still haven't told me or anyone else about what other shit we've got. The worst part is we don't even own this asteroid. We're not armed, and we're about to be attacked, and you want to talk about chain of command protocol like it's the most important goddamn thing we have to do right now, like your rank and your ego are paramount. Well, I've got news for you, ma'am, they're not. I don't care what you did back in the MSS to put all this together. I don't care what you think you're doing now. We need to figure out how to survive this attack. If too many Trogs come to the surface, we're in big trouble."

"You listen to me, you little upstart, nobody officer," her voice is rich with righteous venom.

And with all the surprise anybody would feel who's just spun off the kind of grandiose argument I just slapped her with, I realize my rebuttal-turned-tirade did nothing to win her over to my side.

She goes on to say, "I'm the only reason this revolution is anything right now besides a basement jerk-off fantasy for you and your spaghetti-headed friends. I'm the only reason you're alive, and I'll always be the only reason you stay that way." She reaches out and taps the side of my helmet.

Damn, everybody wants physical contact to make their points today.

"You need to get this through your tantrum-addled brain. It doesn't matter what you think of the Free Army, you're in it now, and we'll maintain our ranks just like the in the SDF. You'll do exactly what the hell I order you to do, or I'll kill switch you and not bat an eye about it. The world is full of starry-eyed revolutionaries who only need to be fostered with half of a freedom dream and a shiny gun. You're nothing special." And to make sure I understand this part, she closes the last centimeters between our faceplates. "You're replaceable."

That confirms it beyond a doubt. Suddenly I'm in the same position I put my platoon in back when we were lifting off from earth and I stood at the end of the compartment and told them I'd kill switch every single one of them if they so much as raised a hand at me.

Goddamn, it makes me feel powerless.

I hate the feeling every bit as much as I've hated my life under the Grays.

"Run out of self-righteous speeches?" sneers Blair.

Yes, however, I'm not a quitter. So, I have more to say. "Whatever you think I am is irrelevant." I nod at some of the troops nearby, steeling themselves for the coming attack. "Their thoughts are important. I wasn't in that prison warehouse with all of you, but I'll bet I know what you talked about. Jill's platoon was with mine when we destroyed those three Trog cruisers over Arizona. That's one hell of a victory, probably the biggest the SDF ever had. It's certainly the biggest thing our paltry rebellion has done in this war. I'll bet all of those soldiers were talking about it and you were egging them on because you had to make them all believe we have a chance to win this."

I see from the look on Blair's face I've hit pay dirt.

"You had to do it, because you couldn't have them thinking this whole thing you led us into was a clusterfuck, or worse, an ambush you baited them into. If they'd started believing that while imprisoned in a Trog warehouse on an asteroid a billion miles from earth with no hope of escape, then they'd have probably had a contest to see who could kill you with their bare hands."

Blair's brain is squirming in a trap of her own making, and she can't find a magic string of bullshit to break herself free. She's not used to being on the losing end of anything. She steps away from me.

It's funny, but I'm too riled up to rudely laugh at her. "The crunchy, nutty icing on your shit cake is this: all those people inside and the ones coming out know it's me and my crew that rescued them. The best part is, because humans are humans, they unfairly ascribe life's complicated achievements to single heroes no matter how many were involved. That's especially true in military matters. Read any history book and you'll know it. The prisoners will say it was me who saved them. Not my platoon. Not what's left of my company. They'll believe it was me who unclustered this fuck-pit you put them in. So, threaten your kill switch all you want. Your hands are tied. If you do it me, these grunts will frag your arrogant ass so fast you'll never see it coming."

Having had plenty of moments now to come up with her rebuttal, Blair snaps back, "Nothing's to stop me from freezing the whole lot of you, and starting from scratch with a new batch."

"Except the only chance you have to not end up as Trog bait is me and these soldiers." Blair is off-balance, and I can see that I've won. "Without me, you have no chance, because whether you like it or not, these soldiers will fight for me and they'll have a chance to win because they believe I can lead them to victory. Nobody believes in you. You're just a bossy MSS cunt that not one of them trusts."

It's my turn to be aggressive. I step up close to Blair so that our faceplates are nearly touching. "So now I'm telling you, ma'am, work with me. Stop pretending this schoolyard posturing is important. You do what you do and be the queen bitch of this whole outfit, and let me do what I need to do—fight these goddamn Trogs and kill 'em."

Chapter 4

Détente.

"I'll work on the defense," I tell Blair. "You get those scout squads out. We won't be staying out here in front of this warehouse any longer than is absolutely necessary."

"What are you going to do to defend it?" asks Blair, looking around at the nooks troops are finding among the rock outcrops and the machinery maze.

"Let's not pretend we're going to get along," I tell her. "Trust me to handle my business. And I'll let you handle your shit."

"Let me?"

I ignore the pettiness. "We'll have plenty of time to bicker when all this is over."

"Ma'am," she spits at me to enforce her authority one more time.

"Fuck you with that shit." I turn and head toward a platoon reconstituting just outside the warehouse door. "Work on assembling the units. And find us a better place than this to defend. We'll all die out here if the Trogs attack in force." I cut my comm link with Blair.

"You," I point, as I walk toward a sergeant who can't hear me. Coming up in front of him, I check his identity and connect with him over the comm while finding his info on my d-pad. I slip his name under my ad hoc unit hierarchy. He looks like he's old enough to be my dad. And now I'm mentally on the other side of the chain of command argument. Ugh, karma. "Around the side of this building, you'll find at least a hundred frozen corpses, all Chinese SDF. Bring them to the front of the warehouse and stack them into ramparts."

"What?" The sergeant is horrified.

"Do it!" Sometimes people need a jolt even if it is rude.

He's looking at my name stencil, and he glances at his d-pad. "Major Kane?"

"That's me."

His attitude changes instantly. He starts to thank me.

"There's a horde of Trogs," I point down the long axis of the Potato. "About a kilometer that way. They're gathering strength for an attack. We need to ready the forces."

"We have no guns," he pleads.

"Work on the ramparts." I look around and spot a handful of soldiers scavenging through one of the mobs of dead Trogs. "I'll have those troops find what weapons they can and bring them to you."

The sergeant looks at the men among the enemy corpses. He scans what he can see of the colony and spots more dead Trogs. His eyes fall on Hastings' body, still lying in the open. He stops there.

With no more command edge in my tone, I tell him, "Do something with her. She's one of us."

He nods, turns to his troops, and starts passing out orders.

I walk toward the scavenging troops, moving a bit slower than I could, and I open a private comm with Phil. "Got a minute?"

"No," he answers.

"You're not doing anything," I tell him, guessing—more than guessing. What could he be up to?

"You don't know that."

"Jesus, Phil. Do you have to make everything difficult?"

"Simple pleasures," he answers.

I sigh. If Phil wasn't so valuable…

"Here's what I need," I tell him. "I need a way to circumvent a kill switch, permanently."

"I don't understand. You've got the kill-switch capability built into your helmet. All you have to do is choose not to activate it."

"That's not what I'm talking about. I'm afraid Blair and I are heading for a major confrontation, and she's already threatened to kill switch me if I don't behave."

"She's a bitch," says Phil, but he's nearly laughing when he says it. He only knows her by name. "That must suck for you, not being in charge."

"Dammit, Phil. This is serious. She can take out everyone in the division, and she thinks we're disposable."

"Disposable?" Now it's Phil's turn to be horrified.

"She thinks she can make her way back to earth for a refill of people just like us, but who are more pliable."

"She can't," argues Phil. "How dumb is she? We've got a bunch of teenagers and middle-aged parents in the ranks now. What comes after that? Geriatrics? Earth is running out of disposable people."

"Exactly." Finally, Phil is engaged in the problem. "What can we do?"

"Switching helmets is the natural solution," he says. "All of the kill switches are coded to the chain-of-command hierarchy. If she has kill-switch authority over the whole division, it won't matter whose helmet you take."

"What about all the Chinese bodies laying stacked beside the warehouse?" I ask. "What are your thoughts?"

"Some of us could swap for those helmets," says Phil, "but are there enough for everyone? Then, whose kill-switch authority are you under? You don't know, do you?"

He's right.

"Maybe she's bluffing," offers Phil. "Have you thought about that?"

Of course, it's possible, but that's an expensive bluff to call.

"If she has a kill switch, then she can listen in on our conversations, too," realizes Phil. "She's probably listening right now."

More Phil drama. Ugh.

Still, he has a point.

I turn and spot Blair in the company of a few sergeants over near the equipment yard, only she isn't looking at them, she's cutting glances at me, and she turns away just as I catch her eye.

Bitch!

I say, "I know you can hear me, Blair."

"What?" cries Phil. "She's actually on the line?"

"Yes," I answer. "Chime in if you want, Blair. I don't care if you know or if you don't. I *will* find a way to disable your kill switch."

"There isn't a way," she tells me, confidently.

"There isn't a *pleasant* way," I answer, thinking back to the small grav plate Captain Milliken placed on my helmet when he was trying to kill me back when this all started. "I'm not interested in harming you. I just want to make sure you don't kill my troops." *Or me.*

Phil mutters something I can't understand, yet I can tell he's frightened.

"Or," I say, "You could trade out your helmet with another, and we'll destroy that one."

"Not on your life," she laughs. The laugh is mean and victorious. She thinks she's got me worried and she thinks she's regaining the upper hand.

"It puts us all on a level playing field," I make my argument, like logic will magically work, "like real soldiers, depending on each other and trusting each other because we share the same values, we fight for the same things. That's how armies succeed, not by threat of death."

"Signing off," says Blair. "I have more important things to do than listening to you two children plot."

"God," says Phil. "She's a bitch."

"Yeah," I agree. "See what you can figure out, okay? In the meantime, I need you and Penny—"

The ground shakes violently as everything flashes bright blue in a grav wash.

I'm knocked onto my back as the comm erupts in shouts.

Chapter 5

The pinprick gleam of a trillion stars hanging in the endless black void is obscured with a giant dirty smudge wrapped in ephemeral blue tentacles.

Jupiter, so prominent in the sky a moment before, is a sideshow of funky rust and dull, gray stripes ornamented with sixty-three moons. The herd of smaller asteroids, stable in their positions relative to the Potato a moment earlier, are all on the move. Some are drifting away. A few inch forward. More are spinning, displaying sharp sparkles as light from our faraway sun catches and reflects away.

A Trog cruiser has inexplicably appeared a kilometer above us. A moment ago there was nothing overhead except vacuum. Now it's there, with plates sucking fusion-drive power and thrashing out repressive grav fields as it stabilizes its two million tons of mass right above us.

The asteroid quakes beneath me.

Every piece of matter within a hundred klicks is reacting to the gravitational perturbations of the cruiser's sudden arrival.

The troops around me see what I'm seeing, and whatever they felt when gravity fluxed and knocked us all off our feet, it's now turning to dread.

How the hell did that Trog cruiser get there?

"It just blipped out of nothing," somebody shouts.

"Oh, Christ," wails another.

Surprising me by how quickly she's collected her wits to rejoin the game, Blair shouts over the comm, "Stand up. Get ready!" They're the right words. Unfortunately, the way she says them, they sound like accusations of cowardice.

"Fucking get ready for what?" somebody mutters.

Still, that cruiser is right there.

It must have come out of bubble jump at that spot, an insanely close place to something as massive as the Potato, an occurrence that shouldn't have been possible, at least not based on what humans understand about grav manipulation.

It's those big-headed gray shits utilizing another talent we humans have no hope of mastering even with a bug in the head.

Then I realize something horrific, my ship is gone.

It was floating in space, just there, near where the bow of the cruiser now occupies the vacuum.

I see some hunks of debris glinting in the sparse light, spinning away from the cruiser's hull.

Oh, my god!

Penny, Phil, and Jablonsky were on the ship.

It's been obliterated by the instantaneous arrival of the Trogs.

I search for my three lookouts that had been a hundred meters above the surface. Lenox in her orange suit should have been easy to spot, yet she's gone. I scan the sky for Silva and Mostyn. They've disappeared as well.

I bounce to my feet as the bug in my head swims through the syrup of so much grav flux. It's disoriented and taking a moment to catch up with the rest of my brain.

I'm looking around, expecting the Trogs from inside the asteroid to be mounting their attack. They're not, not yet. I shore up my guess: They don't have the means to coordinate the arrival of a faster-than-light ship with a ground attack. They have no clocks and no radios—what the hell would they need radios for? Trogs are telepathic like the Grays. At least that's what everyone believes because no one's ever found a radio built into the suit of a dead one.

Nevertheless, we humans only have guesses about the limitations and capabilities of telepathy.

It's time for me to take my cue from Blair's example and get in the game, too. Over the comm link to Blair, I say, "Listen to me. There's no time to muck around. We need to set aside our shit for a minute and get this right. Prep time is done. The battle is here."

Already, I'm too fucking late.

The unmistakable glow of railgun slugs erupts from the tubes along one of the cruiser's spines.

I stop breathing as I watch them come, not even a second passes, because the things fly so damn fast.

The ground around our position explodes with the impact of high-energy metal. Shattered rock spews into the void and tears its way across the asteroid's surface. Orange suits with soldiers inside are punctured and ripped into grotesque shreds of bloody meat frothing blood instantly into the vacuum.

The comm erupts in screams and the rattle of ribs cracking through wrecked chests. It's the sound of hyper-velocity fury finding fragile human bodies. Death in space.

"Max defensive grav!" I shout over the comm. "Max defense!"

The space around us is filling with dust and body parts suspended, drifting, or shooting violently through the chaos.

Dozens are hollering—some orders, some hysterics—sounds obscured by crackling kaleidoscopes of noise from granules of asteroid rock blown off the surface containing the ore of some conductive metal.

"Blair!" I shout, "Blair!" I run through a cloud of gray dust in the direction I last saw her standing. "Blair!" I trip, bounce against a squat stone the size of a couch, and somersault. My defensive grav cushions everything against the asteroid's weak gravity, and I'm back on my feet in a few heartbeats, running, unable to see more than a meter or two ahead.

I leap over a small crater where a railgun round impacted the surface, and I come down on the other side, running until a kneeling figure resolves in the dust storm.

Another salvo pounds the asteroid, and I fall over as hunks of stone pummel me from my left.

I look up and see Blair, still on her knees, hands on the ground, shaking her head, trying to regain her senses.

I jump down in front of her, grab her helmet, and press our faceplates together. "Blair, can you hear me?"

She blinks, and nods.

"Kill all the comms except you, me, and Brice." I can only control my own company's comm links. That's the way our systems come preprogrammed. With my rank and MSS position, I could take control of the equipment of just about any SDF troop in the division, but each control request through my d-pad's interface would have to be done one at a time. Even with my implant, it would take more time than we have.

The comm link is turning into a morale-crushing chaos of sonic horror and preventing every attempt to organize a response.

"Do it!" I shout at Blair.

She reaches slowly to her d-pad.

Dammit!

If only she had a bug in her head like me.

Her fingers tap.

The comm goes dead. It's just me and the static now. "Everyone, listen!"

Listen to what?

What am I going to tell them?

There's only one choice. "We need to retreat underground. We need to do it now. Run to the nearest airlock. Pack yourselves inside, and as soon at it cycles, find your way to the deepest hole in this mining colony."

Blair looks at me with the eyes of a child. Whatever resolve she had a few moments ago, the impacting slugs have shattered it. She's not cut out for war. "It'll cave in," she whines. "We'll be trapped."

"In this g?" I argue. "A cave-in would take a week to seal a tunnel." I hope. Yelling across the deteriorating comm I tell them all, "Head for the lowest subterranean levels, and we'll figure out what to do from there. Go! Go! Go!"

Chapter 6

Gray dust particles, pebbles, and hunks of rock move up, down, sideways, toward me, and away. My eyes try to focus on the bigger pieces, but the crap isn't of a uniform density. Things ghost out of sight and then back in again. The dusky, dim light darkens by the moment. The asteroid's micro-gravity tugs every bit back in the direction of its rocky center, but that'll take days.

If the cruiser keeps up the relentless pounding, they won't have to kill us, we won't be able to see a thing. We won't be a threat.

"Blair." I reach out and grab under the arm and pull her to her feet. "Open up the comm so everyone can talk again. They'll need to work together to follow our orders."

Blair fumbles with her d-pad.

I start dragging her toward the location of the last airlock I saw. It was back near the center of the colony, right where I flew superhero-style into that handful of Trogs that just came out. I guess there has to be a closer airlock. However, with visibility nearing zero, I don't have time for an Easter egg hunt.

Before we've advanced a dozen steps, Blair shakes her arm loose from my grip.

I glance at her. She's straightening her spine, a defiant veneer on her face. Back to boss mode—unlikable, and just the Blair we need.

"Brice," I call over a private comm, hoping there's not so much crap floating between us it'll block the signal. "Are you alright?"

"Trog shit can't kill me," he laughs.

Damn, he's the most twisted man I've ever met. "I'm heading for that dome in the center of the colony."

Another volley of railgun fire slams the asteroid, and I'm back off my feet again.

Blair is down.

A new round of screams tears across the comm.

Slaughter.

"Move as fast as you can away from the warehouse," I tell the troops. "With all the dust, they can't see us, they can only target our last positions." Hopes.

"Was the warehouse hit?" Blair asks me over a private comm.

"Don't know." I can only pray it wasn't—it's a huge target. If the Trogs in that cruiser wanted to destroy the building, nothing would stop them. "How many were still in there?"

"Fifty?" she guesses. "Sixty? A hundred?" Her tone of voice is riding a rollercoaster of emotion she's not used to feeling. "Dammit, I don't know."

I keep her moving. While I think an auto-grav sprint across the asteroid's surface would be the fastest way to get to the airlock, with visibility down to a meter or two, it would be dangerous.

No doubt, the Trogs massing down at the other end of the mining pit are chomping at the bit for the bombardment to stop so they can rush this way and wipe us out while the advantage of our automatic weapons is completely negated.

Over the comm link, I urge everyone to hurry. All I hear in response is unbroken static. Everyone must be too far away.

I trip, yet I don't fall. In asteroid g, falling takes so long I'm only reoriented, looking down at a ground I'll hit in a few days if I let nature take its course, although the ground is not what I see below me. Trog bodies carpet the ground.

"You alright?" Blair asks, whispering unnecessarily. In the silence of space with the eerie fog of rock dust everywhere, a million years of evolution is telling her to be sneaky, and she's doing it in the way a lifetime of earth-borne intuition has taught her.

Reorienting my body with my feet beneath me, I spot the handle of a Trog disruptor blade sticking out from beneath a body. I lean over and pull it by the pommel. Straightening back up, I show it to Blair as I say, "These are the Trogs we killed in the battle before we freed you." Lifting the blade, I reach it out toward her. "Take it. It might come in handy. These things will cut through defensive grav fields like they aren't there."

She accepts it like I've handed her a baggy of warm dog shit, but once her palm wraps around the handle, the disruptor's field lines illuminate in a blue glow—like neon through the dust. She's mesmerized. "Beautiful."

I didn't think she knew any pleasant words. She *must* be in shock.

I point to the blade attached to one of the magnets on my back. "It's a handy place to keep it."

I nod forward. We need to move.

I make my way through the bodies.

She follows, and mounts her blade across her back, clearly more comfortable to have the single-shot Trog railgun in her hands instead.

Another salvo of slugs quake the asteroid.

No screams sound over the comm. It's just me and Blair. She stops walking, taps the side of her helmet, and tries to connect with someone. Anyone but me.

"It's the dust," I tell her. "It's metallic and probably static-charged. It's killing the comm links."

Her grimace pulls tight across her face as she looks at the slow-motion maelstrom around us. I think some of the natural vitriol in her nature is redirecting off of me and into it.

"We need to keep moving," I urge.

She's stopped again, looking back in the direction of the mayhem's epicenter.

Why?

Hell, I don't know.

At first, I think her brain was bounced a little too vigorously inside her skull.

I nudge her. "C'mon."

She doesn't move, except to lean slightly toward the mayhem, like she wants to start walking that way but isn't sure.

I make a new guess, one I can't believe I'm making because it doesn't fit with the black-and-white picture I've painted of her in my mind. There are no hints of empathy and nothing else to make me believe she gave two frog turds about the troops that might still be back by the warehouse.

Is it truly possible she cares about somebody but herself?

I say, "You can't."

She turns and glares some of her silent acid at me.

"There's a fine line between heroism and stupidity," I tell her.

"I'm not—"

"Use your head," I go on, half torn between doing exactly what I'm advising her not to do. "We can't know how many are moving toward the airlocks now, but we know some of them are headed that way—probably most, maybe all." If ever there was a hope turned into words on nothing but a handful of vacuum, that's it. "We made a plan." Not exactly *we*. "We announced it to everybody. We need to stick with it."

I turn and trudge forward, hoping she follows. Well, half-hoping.

As the gray dust flows past my glass faceplate, I wonder, how many more of my platoon are dead? What do those stats look like now?

Chapter 7

I don't know how long we've been walking, except 'too long' is a phrase echoing in my head.

The bombardment seems to have ceased.

The dust around us is thinning the further our feet churn us away from the target zone. I can make out shapes as far as ten feet away. Nothing to brag about, but better than arm's length.

Puffs of dust, thicker than the surrounding murk, move through the gray haze like ghosts, putting me on edge. I keep my railgun at my shoulder while I'm looking down the barrel, ready to destroy anything that might be a Trog.

"Do you know where we are?" asks Blair.

We passed the stocky stone spire not long after finding Blair's salvaged disruptor, and we haven't come across anything in what seems like too long of a time. Just dust. It's easy to imagine we're lost in an endless fog.

I should have checked the time on my d-pad before we started. With adrenaline flooding my circulatory system, with near-complete sensory deprivation, low g, little light, and no sound but Blair's angry wheeze, I feel decoupled from reality. We may have been walking a minute or twenty. I honestly don't know.

"Are you going to answer?" Blair pushes.

"Can't say." We should have arrived at the circular structure in the center of the colony already. *It seems like we should have.* If not that, then something. Hell, we could be moving in circles for all I know. I chuckle. At least we won't walk off the edge of the Potato, though we might circumnavigate it.

Magellan Kane and The Sourpuss Queen, explorers extraordinaire!

"What's funny?"

"Nothing." I glance at the ground, looking for footprints and shuffle marks. My footprints. Blair's shuffle. She's more careful about foot placement than me.

Blair calls over the open comm again, searching for anyone who might hear.

A voice tries to respond, sounding like sixty-percent static and thirty-percent gargle spit.

Ten percent more of whatever.

"You make any of that out?" she asks.

"No."

"It sounded like two or three different people to me." It could have been a recording of crunching tinfoil for all I could distinguish.

"We should try another direction." Like most of the things Blair says, her suggestion carries too much certainty.

"Take the lead," I tell her. "I'll admit. I'm lost." It's easier than igniting another argument. I stop walking and look back at her.

She's hesitating.

"What?" I ask.

"I don't know which direction," she spits it like I've accused her of misdirecting us. "There doesn't seem to be anything this way."

"There should be," I tell her, some of my frustration escaping through my words. "There's a whole damn mining colony here, twenty or thirty structures. We should have run into a wall or something."

"This doesn't make any sense," she mutters.

"Most problems don't," I explain, "until they're solved."

"Did you get that from a fortune cookie?"

Sarcastic enthusiasm seems like the right choice. "No fortune cookie ever lied to me." I start walking again. "Keep an eye on the ground. Look for our tracks in the dust."

"Our tracks?" She doesn't immediately guess why.

I decide not to fill her in. She'll conclude soon enough that I'm a circle-walking idiot.

Thankfully, for whatever reason, she keeps them to herself.

We trudge.

Frustration builds.

Minutes pass, and I stop to look up, hoping to see something to help me figure out where I am. I see more dark dust with the black of space behind it, and I see the rough glow of the Trog ship transforming the haze into a brighter color. At least we're still on the same side of the asteroid as the colony, unless the cruiser has moved into orbit around the Potato.

"What are you thinking?" asks Blair.

"Maybe taking off and flying above this shit to see where we are."

"We're lost then?"

Like it was a mystery. Still, I don't jump.

She doesn't take the opportunity to pounce on me to vent her frustration over our situation.

I don't thank her for making the effort to keep her vitriolic shit to herself. In the few dozen hours since she and I first met, we already have too much history between us to make kindness easy.

After a patient moment, she asks, "What's the hesitation?"

"Variables. Too many."

"Like?"

"What if the Trogs in that cruiser spot me and decide we're all still alive down here and start firing again?"

Blair groans. "Look at me."

I do. Her face shows a lot more frustration than she's voicing.

"Not at my face." She spreads her arms and steps back.

I can't guess where she's going with this. I look at her chest. Pointless. Through the suit, I can't make out anything of her femininity.

"Not my tits, you dumbass. I'm covered in this damn dust. So are you. If you fly up there to get above it, nobody on that ship will see you, you'll be the same color as this cloud.

I shake my head. If she had a bug in her head, she'd know. "It's not the Trogs I'm worried about. They have Grays on that ship."

"Why them?" she asks.

I give her the briefest rundown of what I saw on the cruiser my platoon commandeered, emphasizing the number of Grays we saw in the command section. I remind her that Phil sensed more of them on the Potato, somewhere down in the tunnels. I finally tell her, "I don't know if the Trogs and Ticks are allies or what, but if I grav up there, to one of those big-headed gargoyles I'll glow like a Roman candle. The dust won't hide my grav signature."

Blair's shoulders slump. She understands. "Let's walk, then. We're bound to find something. This rock isn't that big."

I press on.

She follows.

She tries to raise the others on the comm again. Louder bursts of static are the only thing we hear.

I scan the moving slurry around us for any hint of a structure.

More minutes pass, I guess. I still didn't check the time on my d-pad. "How long have we bee—"

I freeze.

"What?" asks Blair, concerned, and rightly so.

"Shhh." Pointless. I remind myself again, sound doesn't carry in a vacuum.

I watch as the dust ahead of me takes on a different texture—puffs with sharp edges, dark clouds.

Blair nudges me and whispers over the comm, "What?"

A few meters ahead, shapes are moving, left to right, and the bug in my head helps me see the dense mass of each. It's not dust.

"Trogs," I tell her, still stuck on the unnecessary whisper. "Back up."

Instead, Blair leans to look past me, and I bump her as I step back.

She's not moving. "I can't see them."

Scooting around beside her, I grab her arm and pull her down to her knees, pointing with my rifle. "You can barely make them out. They're filing by. Watch. You can see faint shapes."

Leaning forward, Blair says, "Kind of. I think I can see them. God, you have good eyes."

Mostly it's my sense of gravity. "Don't move."

"We could have run right into them."

"Yeah." I'm trying to detect the end of the line, hoping it's not that whole Trog horde coming this way.

"What next?" Blair asks, softly, humbly, as hard as it is for her to step off her ego pedestal for a moment.

I think.

Retreat?

Find another way in?

Oh, fuck it!

It's been a day of insane risks. I spot what looks like the last in the line of them, although for all I know it might be just a gap. Frustration over our current mess reinvigorates the anger I have toward the Trogs for the bombardment, and it's time to vent it. "I'm going to fucking kill them."

Blair shrieks, "What?"

It always amuses me how much meaning can be packaged around a simple syllable. Human language is so interesting.

I'm up and on my feet, letting go of my rifle and drawing my pistol as I move toward the last Trog in line. "Stay right behind, Blair. If I lose you out here, I won't find you again."

"This is a bad idea." She's angry. "You'll get us killed!"

"Unless we can figure out a way to turn this shit sandwich into a Salisbury steak, we're dead anyway."

"What the hell are you talking about?"

"Just be ready with that rifle if this goes south."

"If?" She scoffs. "If?"

She says more, however, I'm ignoring her. I'm straining to feel the grav of any humanoid masses moving nearby. All I see is the line of Trogs stretching out in front of me as I fall into step.

They're walking close, just far enough away from one another so the one behind won't kick the heels of the one in front when they step.

Second thoughts and pictures of all that could go wrong start to spin in a flurry of nerves as my mouth goes dry, but I can't pay attention to any of that. All the best shit only works if you jump right in.

I shuffle my feet to match the rhythm of their march. In long strides, I close in on my target.

As I get in range, he senses something and turns to glance over his shoulder.

Dammit!

The telepathic fucker probably caught a sniff of my bug.

I reach out and grab his integrated backpack with one hand while I jam my pistol just under the metal ring attaching his helmet to his suit. I pull the trigger and send a slug up through the base of his big bony skull.

He stiffens and pitches forward from the momentum of the projectile smashing inside his helmet. My grip is tight on his backpack, and he doesn't fall. In the micro-g, I hold him up in front of me, and pray the next Trog in line is feeling just as much sensory overload as I am, and doesn't sense his buddy's demise.

Nothing happens further ahead that I can make out.

I fling the dead Trog's body to the side, and tell Blair, "Make sure he doesn't bounce." In the light-g, it *will* happen, and the last thing I want is the Grays on that cruiser to start seeing Trog bodies springing into orbit. No doubt, that would prompt them to start pounding us again with their railguns.

I grab the pack on the back of the next Trog in line, place my pistol, pull my trigger, and toss his body to the side for Blair to handle.

It can't be this easy.

Chapter 8

Eight down, and even Blair is impressed.

It's a great system. I ambush and shoot. She handles the corpses. What's not to love?

I'm starting to think we should forget about finding an airlock and just stay out here in the gray slurry, hunting and killing.

I skip my feet to get in step with the leader of a line that doesn't exist anymore, except for him and me, and as I adjust my stride to catch up, I'm in a rhythm.

He stops.

Shit!

Panicking, thinking my system just fell apart in a puddle of hubris and that I should move my pistol back up into firing position, I plow into him from behind, and it feels like I've bumped into a tree.

The Trog half turns and elbows me hard on the side of the helmet.

My defensive grav absorbs the shock, yet the momentum nearly knocks me off my feet.

Blair is shouting and bringing her rifle to bear.

The Trog doesn't turn all the way around. He focuses forward again, not realizing the frail dust-covered moron behind wasn't one of his comrades.

Confused about that for a half-second as I regain my balance, I realize the Trog has just pressed his palm into the center of a backlit pad with only one big button.

An airlock door slides open.

"Blair, don't shoot yet!"

"Why?"

Lights flicker on inside. I shout, "Airlock!" and rush in after the Trog.

I'm too slow.

As I'm getting close enough to put the barrel of my pistol in the best spot to kill him, he reaches the inner door and turns to check that the rest of the squad has followed. His oversized eyes betray his surprise, whether because he sees only two dust-covered suits instead of eight, or because he recognizes me as human, I don't know.

I'm already pushing forward and trying to shove the barrel of my pistol up under his chin.

He blocks me with a forearm that's longer and more muscular than mine.

Before I can adjust and pull my pistol free, he's wrapping a powerful ape hand around my wrist and squeezing so hard I lose control of my fingers.

Through his faceplate, I see his surprise is gone, replaced by bared teeth.

He pushes me to my knees.

My God, he's strong.

I'm struggling with all my might and way overmatched. I figure in a few moments, I'll be dead.

I amp up my suit grav to push him away and find some leverage. He instantly responds.

"Double shit!"

A railgun barrel slides unexpectedly over my shoulder and past my helmet, stopping when it pokes the Trog in the chest. It fires as soon as the barrel makes contact.

Too close for the Trog's suit grav to protect him, the dinner-plate-sized deflector over his sternum explodes in a burst of shrapnel and hits my faceplate as all the air from his lungs bursts free. For the briefest of seconds, I see a hole form straight through him as Blair's round sparks against the airlock's interior door.

The grip on my wrist relaxes, and a bubbly fountain of bloody air sprays out.

I push the Trog away, and he floats up toward the ceiling.

Blair is punching the button to close the outer door. "You alright?"

"Yeah." I rub my forearm and flex my fingers. Nothing broken. "Damn, he was strong."

"First time one got his hands on you?"

I look at her like it's a stupid question.

The outer door seals.

She shrugs. "How am I supposed to know what happened when you went all Blackbeard on those Trog cruisers. You could have arm-wrestled them for control."

Attempted humor? From Blair?

"No hand-to-hand." Standing up, I scan the airlock's inner door for a hole left by Blair's shot. "If I have anything to say about it in the future, it won't happen again."

"That strong?" Blair walks the length of the airlock to punch the button by the inner door to cycle the atmosphere back inside.

I'm still examining the door for a hole as I hear a high-pitched hiss. Air is filling in around me.

"Don't worry." More of her irritating certainty. "The round didn't go through."

Chapter 9

The airlock stops hissing. A light above the door turns green. We're matched for the pressure inside.

Blair has a palm on the door handle. She looks at me for confirmation.

Who am I kidding? She wants me to know she's going to open and it and I better be ready.

With my rifle set to full auto, I'm prepared to kill however many of whatever is behind door number one. I nod my response.

The inner door swings open and I take a quick step forward for a full view.

I scan left to right.

Upturned and scattered are lounge chairs, the kind you might find by a pool back on earth—not now, but the kind in old movies when people with enough meat on their bones to look alluring in a swimsuit would sun themselves by the blue water and demurely try to get laid.

Clearly, the Trogs didn't appreciate the arrangement of the chairs and tables.

We're under the big smart-glass dome at the center of the colony, right where we intended to be. The main floor is down a short flight of wide stairs coming out of the airlock. Along the top edge of the circular wall supporting the dome's glass, dim lights glow in a ring broken by dead and flickering sections. Doorways are set at irregular intervals around the perimeter, each opening to downward stairs and obscured hallways.

In the center of the circular room rises a fountain of the same shape. At first, I think it's filled with an unfamiliar super-viscous liquid. That damned earth-borne intuition again. The goo is actually water flowing in the micro-g, with droplets falling so slowly they seem to be suspended in the air. Vertical waves, several feet tall and narrow, crawl around the fountain's inside edge, not collapsing, but standing and morphing ever so slowly into mesmerizing, impossible shapes.

Impossible back on earth.

"There!" Blair points.

I swing my rifle and find a target.

I don't pull the trigger.

The suit is orange, not white. The helmet is normal, human with a high forehead. His uniform, as grimy as any of the worn-out suits most of us wear, isn't layered in the asteroid's dust. That means he wasn't outside when the bombardment started.

But there's no Korean name and rank stenciled on his chest. He's not military.

"Who are you?" I demand, sending a signal across all the standard comm channels, and looping Blair in. I step down the stairs. Blair follows.

"SDF?" he lies.

"Who are you?" I demand, taking a step forward and jabbing the barrel of my railgun in his direction, even while I'm thinking what a stupid gesture it is—*Oh, looky, in case you didn't notice, here's my big fucking gun.*

"Tarlow," he answers. He's cagey. Just a pinch shorter than me. Not at all intimidating. He reminds me of a real live Teddy Bear. I have an inexplicable urge to hug him. He glances at the airlock up the stairs behind us like maybe he thinks if he makes a dash for the door, he'll move so fast all my shots will miss.

I don't need hugs today. I'm ready to play.

Maybe he guessed at the thoughts behind my eyes. He doesn't run. Instead, he asks, "The Trogs?"

"Still out there," Blair tells him. "Who are you? Are you one of the miners?"

He glances down at his suit and then back to us as if that's a sufficient answer.

I'm thinking maybe I'll just shoot him. Something's not right about him, and the more I get comfortable with the act of ending lives, the less it seems like it'll be a burden on my conscience to erase this cuddly irritant.

Blair hops off the final stair and stomps across the big circular rec area like maybe she's about to slap some MSS-super-interrogation-shit on him. Clearly, she has no patience for Mr. Cuddles, either.

It's surprising how little crap you'll put up with when sixty seconds ago you were fighting for your life.

I ease to the side, so Blair isn't in my line of fire.

As she closes in, I see Tarlow's smirk slip into something a little less confident. I figure he's reading the hostility on her face, and filling his suit's recycler. His hands fly up with open palms and his scruffy beard parts wide to reveal a glowing, toothy smile.

I wonder how long it's been since he was last out of his suit.

I shudder over the idea of my future spending every day in a flexible orange coffin.

"I'm not one of the miners," he says. "I'm a tech. A jack-of-all-trades. A gopher. I fix things."

"Like what?" Blair demands, from just a step out of fist-punching range.

"Everything." With Blair stationary, some of Tarlow's new-found deference disappears and he looks at Blair like the question is nearly too stupid to expound on. His eyes drift down to the single-shot rifle still in her hands. He doesn't know she failed to chamber another round after she killed the Trog manhandling me in the airlock.

Come to think of it, I'm not sure Blair knows either.

Maybe she had time to work the bolt action, but I didn't see her do it.

"We're on a rock a billion miles past bumfuck-nowhere," snorts Tarlow. "We're running an illegal mining operation. We can't exactly call back to earth for a repairman when something breaks. I fix everything."

"Nobody fixes everything," I retort. I decide he's lying.

He looks past Blair, and sees me sighting my rifle at the center of his chest. Whatever the stabbing thing I did with the railgun a moment before didn't convey, apparently my demeanor does now. He gulps. "I don't fix the mining machinery, not much of it. Well, the kilns sometimes, and the small-scale smelters. I support other systems, air purifiers, electrical lines, radio repeaters, networking, lights." He gestures at the malfunctioning illumination along the edges of the glass dome, just in case we don't know what a fucking light is. "Oh yeah, explosives, you know, for blasting rock. I mix the chemicals and set up the charges before they drop them down into the drill holes."

Blair relaxes. She seems to have gleaned an answer she deems sufficient. "What happened here?"

I keep my rifle up. I'm not that trusting.

"Trogs." With Blair's aggression dialed back a notch, Tarlow cranks an extra helping of disdain back into his answer. "You said they were outside."

"They attacked the base?" Blair asks.

"Base?" Tarlow shuffles back a step as he glances at the SDF stencils on Blair's chest. "Who said base?"

Blair exaggerates a sigh and glares back at me. She's out of patience.

"Stop being evasive!" I order. *What the heck?* Blair was going to say it anyway.

"I know this is a Free Army base," she tells him. "That's why *we're* here. You know it's a Free Army base or *you* wouldn't be here. Can we please skip the secret handshake game? Tell me what the hell happened and tell me why you're freely wandering around with Trogs everywhere, because I have to tell you Mr. Fix-it, with every stupid answer you give me, you're convincing me you're a collaborator who needs to have a round punched through his chest." Blair lunges forward and jams the barrel of her empty railgun between Tarlow's ribs. "Answers. Fast."

Chapter 10

"I... I..." Tarlow is looking at me, eyes pleading. *The bitch is crazy!*

Duh!

Maybe it's a mistake, but I now feel sorry for him. I transition from orders to advice. "Really, stop being evasive." He's rattled, and I'm guessing the answers will come slower. That's probably rationalization.

"I'm not being evasive." He's stumbling over his words. "They've got everyone locked up—the ones they didn't kill."

"Where?" asks Blair.

"Level nine?" Tarlow points down. "In some of the empty reservoirs."

"Reservoirs?" I ask. That word doesn't seem to fit with our current environment.

Tarlow looks at me like I should know the answer to that question already. "It's why the Trogs came here."

"Because of reservoirs?" Blair doesn't understand, either. She thinks Tarlow is spinning up some bullshit.

"Water," Tarlow pronounces. "The rock in this asteroid is hydrous, thirty-nine billion tons of stone soaked with a billion tons of H_20."

Blair is taken aback. "Water?"

The water comment throws me off too.

"Frozen," Tarlow tells us. "We mine it out of the core, extract it from the rock, and store it in subterranean reservoirs —big tanks down on level nine until we ship it out to the other mining colonies. It's the main thing we dig for out here. I think that's why the Trogs came. There aren't that many water mines in the asteroid belt."

"Or they happened upon a colony and decided to attack." Blair is being argumentative. She's probably wired that way, someone who disagrees when progress is as easy as shutting up and listening.

"None of that matters," I tell them both, comprehending what I see is the real news. "The Trogs didn't destroy the base. They captured it. They took prisoners. Blair, the assault ship crews weren't the only ones." Refocusing on Tarlow, I ask, "How many are down there?"

"No." Blair disagrees, of course. "What's important is how Tarlow got out when it seems nobody else did."

"I wasn't locked up," he argues, hurrying to the next part. "I was never captured. I know all the nooks and crannies. How to override the systems. I knew where to hide when the Trogs occupied the base."

"And why are you wandering around, now?" asks Blair.

"The Trogs all of a sudden hurried away." He points to the far end of the Potato. "Down the halls leading to the gun emplacements. I figured it was my chance to make my way to the surface and steal the tug."

"That's why you're wearing the suit," I deduce.

"I've been in the suit for two months."

"To abandon your friends." Blair doesn't try to hide her disgust for his behavior.

"No." Tarlow shakes his head vigorously. "No."

That answer's clearly not true, and I have the urge to tell him he should think through his lies before he starts to spout them, but where would the fun be in that?

Blair pokes him hard in the ribs a few more times. "You're a coward, Tarlow. You were planning to run off, weren't you?"

Shaking his head, Tarlow says, "I…I… maybe. I don't know. I had to get away. I'd have sent back help. I would have." He's convincing himself now. Trying to, anyway.

"The tug is gone," says Blair. "Even if it wasn't, there's a Trog cruiser parked about a klick up. It would've blasted the tug into junk before you made it ten meters off the ground."

"Just one?" asks Tarlow. "Two attacked us."

"We destroyed one," I tell him.

He looks at me, wide-eyed, a hopeful smile starting to form. "You brought the fleet?" And then he looks sick. "I thought you weren't SDF."

"No," I tell him, "there's no fleet. Let's get back to the important stuff. How many Trogs were down here? Where are the Grays? How many of you are locked up on level nine? Where did the Trogs put the weapons they took from you when you surrendered?"

Tarlow gawks at me. "How do you know about the Grays?"

"I got a postcard about it." My impatience for answers I'm not getting is starting to irritate me.

"From who?"

"Kane's being an ass," Blair tells him. "How many Trogs?"

Tarlow reaches up to scratch his beard, remembers his helmet is there, and instead stares at the glass dome above us. After a moment, he says, "A thousand, maybe."

"Weapons?" she asks. "Where are they?"

"Weapons?"

"The ones they took from my troops?"

"In one of the surface buildings, I think." Tarlow looks up and to his left. "I haven't found them, and I've looked. Unfortunately, with a thousand Trogs, it's hard to sneak around."

"How many of you are there?" asks Blair, finally getting back around to my question.

"Four hundred and sixty-nine," he answers, "In three reservoirs."

"That's pretty exact." Blair is skeptical. "How'd you manage to count them if they were all locked up and you weren't?"

It's Tarlow's turn to be taken aback by her stupidity.

I figure it's best not to say anything at this point, lest I suffer a withering glance as well.

Tarlow points to a small round module mounted on one of the walls. A green LED glows near one edge. "Signal relays. We've got them all through the tunnels. They carry the standard bands supported by the comm systems in the helmets. We need the relays because of the metals in the ore screwing up the signals. Otherwise, we wouldn't be able to communicate down here."

"How many of the four-sixty-nine are military, and how many are miners?" I ask.

"Mostly miners and support personnel," answers Tarlow. "The garrison went out to fight the Trogs on the surface when they arrived. They were wiped out. The survivors surrendered."

"Trogs don't usually take prisoners," says Blair. "How'd that work?"

"We were all underground when the fighting ended," continues Tarlow. "The Grays found a way to telepathically link to one of the control room spaghetti-heads. They forced her to tell the commander to surrender, or they'd bomb us to dust. What else could we do?"

"Do you know why they took you prisoner?" asks Blair.

Of course, she and the other SDF mutineers were taken prisoner as well. Maybe that's the question she's really getting at.

Tarlow shrugs. "I don't know if they were going to make us work the mine for them or take us back to Troglandia—"

I laugh.

Blair glares at me. "What?"

"That's what I call it in my inner voice, *Troglandia*. Seriously." I stop laughing, because Blair is looking at me as if she wants to come over and poke me with her empty railgun. "It's funny, right?"

She clearly doesn't appreciate my humor.

She turns back to Tarlow.

He straightens up and glances at us both, like he's going to make an important announcement. "If Grays are in charge of the Trogs, like they're in charge of the earth, maybe the Trogs' Grays decided to acquire some human breeding stock to supplement their slave pool. Maybe that's why they changed their policy on taking prisoners."

CHAPTER 11

Behind me, the airlock door clinks against its frame.

I jump.

The light mounted above it flashes red.

Tarlow's eyes go wide, and he starts backing toward one of the doorways to the lower levels.

"Don't move," Blair orders.

"But..." Tarlow points at the airlock, ignoring Blair's admonition not to move.

I'm already against the wall, pulling one of the upturned lounge chairs in front of me.

"Railgun slugs will go right through that," Tarlow bawls.

"I don't want it to protect me." Why am I explaining myself to Tarlow? "I just want it to *hide* me long enough for them to make it inside so I can take 'em out all at once."

"We should go down to level three," Tarlow tells us. "I have a place down there—"

Blair pushes him through one of the doors and Tarlow stumbles on the stairs. "Get down," she tells him, "and stay." She kneels, using a wall for cover, and levels her weapon at the airlock door.

"You might want to chamber a round," I suggest. "You're too used to the automatic you had."

"Shit." She fumbles with the railgun made for larger Trog hands.

"Not loaded?" Tarlow groans as he steps back.

I swing the barrel of my gun around to put him in my sights. "Don't."

"We're on the same side," Blair tells him. "Stop being such a chicken-shit."

"I don't have a gun."

The light above the door turns to yellow.

"Air's going back in," whines Tarlow. "We can still run."

Full of confidence from the nine Trogs I killed—well, maybe eight—on the way here, I think I'm good. "How many will fit in there? Eight? Ten if they pack tight?"

"Yes," Tarlow answers, "but they usually go in six at a time. They have a fetish for that number, just like the Grays."

"You know a lot about them," Blair observes.

"I've been watching them for two months," replies Tarlow.

"Two months?" It doesn't seem possible. Pointing out the hole in his story, I say, "How could you keep watch on them for two months and not get caught?"

"The camera system, of course."

I glance at Tarlow.

He's pointing again.

I follow the line of his finger and see a small, unobtrusive lens attached above one of the exit doors.

"They're all over the complex," he says.

Blair asks, "How do you—"

The light above the airlock turns green. The door unseals and swings open.

I press against the wall, thankfully cut from asteroid stone, exactly the color I'm coated in. With the lights flickering dim to add to my advantage, I doubt I'll be spotted. I brace myself to pull the trigger.

Gray-dusted figures enter—one, and two more.

They stop on the stairs, glancing around as the airlock seals behind them.

They're carrying rifles. Their bodies aren't thick like Trogs. Their helmets are shaped and sized for human heads.

I don't fire.

The one in front turns and looks right at me. "If you're trying to ambush a Trog, do it from the right." It's Brice. "Nearly all of them are left-handed."

"What?" How the hell did he spot me so easily?

"And the lights," says Brice. "The dimness doesn't do you any good. Ever notice how Trogs have those big puppy dog eyes? Well, it means they see pretty damn good in the dark. You're better off turning the light all the way up and making them squint."

"How the hell come nobody ever told us this shit in training?" I stand up and smile, despite feeling somewhat humiliated for my failed ambush.

Walking down the stairs and into the room, Brice ignores the question. He doesn't have the answer. It's those damn North Koreans who write the SDF curriculum.

He and the other two are near the center of the room when I join them. Blair is dragging Tarlow out of his hiding place to come toward us.

"Took forever to get here," says Brice. "Dust and rocks floating everywhere and Trogs all over the place. Hell, I even tripped on a few."

Blair glances at me like it's my fault and I'm thinking she should be singing my praises, not assigning blame for someone tripping.

Brice catches the glance and looks at me, too.

I shrug. "I've whacked eight outside. Blair killed one in the airlock."

"You're full of surprises, Kane. I'll give you that." Brice turns to Tarlow. "Who's this?"

"A local," I answer, before giving Brice and the two soldiers with him the quickest rundown I can manage.

"What's the plan, then?" asks Brice. "With all the debris in the air, I think the Trogs will be out there a while trying to find us." He looks around. "It's not a huge asteroid, but it'll take a couple of hours at least."

Tarlow steps forward, stammers, and then says, "When the Trogs attacked last time, they pounded us with railguns before disembarking their horde. It took a week for decent visibility to return up top and another few weeks for most of the broken rock to settle back down to the surface."

"Well they won't be out there for three weeks, that's for sure." Brice glances at Blair, then his eyes settle on me.

I start to speak, and Blair, suddenly back in MSS Colonel mode, talks right over me. "The group we killed was heading into the airlock. So no guarantees they'll be out there a long time. Not all of them, anyway."

Into her pause, I blurt, "We need to get this show on the road." They all look at me, and why not? I said it with the confidence of someone who has a plan. After a quick spin on my brain's imagination wheel, I come up with one. "Tarlow, can we access that video feed for all the internal cameras? How do we connect our SDF suit comms to the internal relay system?"

"Passcode for the comm," says Tarlow, again like it was a question so stupid it was barely worth his breath to answer. After some pained sighs, he provides it.

Like the others, I power up my d-pad to enter the code. Thankfully, the temperamental little device decides it's abused our relationship enough for one day, and accepts the numerals without error.

Looking up, Blair has hers ready to go.

Brice is pissed. His d-pad is on the fritz.

Turning to Tarlow and tapping my d-pad, I ask, "Can you fix these things, too? Mine doesn't work half the time."

He nods. "It takes a while," he says. "There are plenty up top on those dead Chinese. Theirs always work."

I doubt the Chinese have any better equipment than we do, but I don't say anything about it.

Tarlow continues, "Your best bet is to switch yours out for one of theirs."

"Only it's integrated with the suit," I argue. "How do you switch it?"

"I could do it," he answers. "But it would take a while. And then you'd have to reprogram it and it—"

"Takes a while?" I guess, with a big eye roll.

Neither of the troops who came in with Brice can get their equipment to respond to the passcode.

"What about camera access?" asks Blair.

"The room I've been hiding out in is on sublevel three," says Tarlow, "I tapped into the camera feed and set up some monitors to watch."

"That's it, then," I announce. I point to the two soldiers who came in with Brice. "You two, go with Blair and Tarlow and get down to that room. Keep on eye on Tarlow." I turn to Brice. "We'll hit the other airlocks and collect any survivors who make it inside." Looking back to Blair, I see she's pissed again, now that I'm passing out orders. "We'll send them your way.

Thankfully, she doesn't pick a new fight.

"Tarlow," I ask, "how do I find my way around this complex?"

"I've been taking all the maps off the walls," he says sheepishly. "The Trogs understand the pictures. They're not stupid." He shrugs. "I left the written signs up. They can't read."

"Not our language, anyway."

"They can't read at all," he argues.

Jesus! Some people have to be obstinate about everything.

"So airlock signs?" asks Brice. "On the walls?"

"Hanging from the ceiling at hallway intersections." Tarlow cocks his head toward one of the interior doors. "Each has an arrow showing the way."

I tell Brice, "That'll be good enough to start with." Turning back to Tarlow, I ask, "Which way to the nearest airlock?"

He points through one of the doorways. "Down that way, third left. About a hundred meters. There's no sign marking that one."

"Great." Brice starts to go.

"When I get down to my computer," says Tarlow, "I can send a map to your d-pad. Look for the message to come through."

"Good." Looking back to Blair as I follow Brice, I say, "Once you're in front of the monitors, you'll need to direct us to whichever airlock our troops come through."

"I know how to do my job, Major." She raises her voice for the next part, so it's clear to all of us it's an order. "Get moving."

Chapter 12

Brice and I are in a featureless hall cut through the asteroid's stone. Technically, it's a tunnel, but not what I'd imagine a mining tunnel to look like. Each wall is flat and straight, set at right angles with the ceiling and floor. The long corridor we ran down to get here, this hall, and the one we saw on the way, look pretty much like any hall in a large building back on earth. Like a hospital, in fact, with floors ground smooth and colored a light gray. Only the rough texture and pale whitewash inadequately masking the natural color of the stone walls give away the secret that you're underground.

We've come to a stop in a twenty-meter-long stub of a passage branched off the main corridor. All it contains is an airlock door, right at the end. The door isn't open. No light is on above to indicate it's being used. None of our troops is standing in the hall, uninjured and happy to see us.

I stare at the door as I shuffle closer to it, willing it to open, wanting to see someone from my platoon come through.

"My dog used to do that," says Brice. "Stare at his food bowl when he was hungry, like maybe looking at it would magically fill it up."

Unable to come up with a clever retort, I look back down the way we came.

"Not a speck of anything to hide behind," says Brice.

"Back to the main hall?" I'm not sure what to do. My hopes were pinned too tightly to the prospect of our troops being here, awaiting direction.

He shrugs. "No cover there, either."

I start walking back. "We'll keep an eye on the light over the airlock door. From the corner, we can watch the main hall, too."

"Good enough." Brice follows along, glancing over his shoulder in case the airlock light should change color.

The floor shakes and I hear a rumble through the air in the hall.

I look up. "Still bombing us?"

"Or our troops setting off charges," says Brice. "Those explosions are too big for them to be hand grenades."

Two more explosions quake through the floor.

I call over the comm. "Blair, progress?"

"On level three," she tells me. "Trogs are down here, however, they haven't seen us."

"Can you get to Tarlow's video room?"

"He says yes."

"You need our help with those Trogs?" Still disappointed about not finding any of our soldiers, I'm considering abandoning my plan to sweep the airlocks.

"Too many," she tells me. "Two guns won't make a difference."

I don't agree. Brice and I have automatic weapons. She and the two troops with her are carrying ill-fitting Trog antiques.

Antiques? I suppress a laugh at that thought. Our forces were using pretty much the same railguns until our two heavy assault divisions launched with the new weaponry yesterday morning.

Brice takes up a position at the corner where the two halls meet. He's in the branch hall and scanning back and forth down the main corridor.

I stand at the opposite corner, keeping an eye on the airlock. "How long should we wait?"

"As long as it takes."

Disappointed with his answer, I tell him, "You've been in this shit before. Is that all you've got—vague bullshit?"

"Get used to it. This isn't a training sim with multiple choice answers anymore." His dismissiveness seems a little harsh. Drilling his hard eyes through my faceplate, he says, "I'll apologize if you want me to."

I roll my eyes and look down his hall. "Isn't there supposed to be some kind of camaraderie between men who've gone to war together?"

Brice rolls out another of his bleak chuckles. "Maybe I'm out of practice. Maybe I'm not in the mood." He rescans his hall and glances back toward the airlock door. "Everybody dies."

I nod, conversationally, out of habit, polite agreement, I don't know. I stop, and I start ticking through the numbers in my head again. *Holy mother of flaming dog shit!* I don't know if anybody in my company is still alive.

Maybe everybody *does* die.

Phil and Penny, my two best friends are dead.

Wait.

There's Jill. Perhaps she's it. The portion of her platoon not killed in the cruiser assault is all that's left of my command.

"See," says Brice.

I look up from wherever my eyes had wandered. Brice is scrutinizing me.

"See?" he repeats. "Something in your brain triggers when they start dying by the dozen. Like the emotion meter redlines and blows a fuse, so you forget to feel it. That's how you keep moving."

I'm not sure that's true. It keeps coming up and bothering me. I thought the numbers were a refuge from the emotion, but I find the dismal death counts turning on me.

"When you stop and breathe," he says. "When you take a minute to stare at a door that doesn't open, when you have time to sleep, when you're in a platoon compartment looking at forty faces that will all soon be dead, those are the times when it comes back, the memories, the emotions. They'll ruin you as a soldier if you let them. In the quiet times, you have to deal with that shit in your head. When you do, it hurts. Blown fuses are easier."

Brice looks up and down each of the halls again.

"How many have died under your command?" I regret asking even as the last syllable crosses the comm link between us.

For the tiniest of moments, his eyes look glassed with tears—that passes with a blink, and a face turned hard. "I stopped counting when I stopped sleeping."

"How do you deal with it?" I'm still trying to tally the number of dead who followed my orders to their end.

"I don't have any Freudian hoodoo, if that's what you're asking."

I glance away. It was what I was asking.

"I'm wired for it," says Brice, "I guess, as much as anybody who's not a sociopath. I handle it. Yeah, I lose sleep. I'm angry sometimes for no good reason." And then his laugh flows out, black as tar, sticky and hot. "And fragging a shitbird officer without a blink of remorse. There's no justice in this war, on our planet, perhaps not anywhere in the whole damn universe. Maybe justice is a fantasy backward civilizations like ours think is real, like sun gods and fairies. I don't know." He takes a deep breath. "When I pulled that trigger and plugged Captain Milliken, for just a second there, justice existed. It made some of the shit better."

I nod, not out of courtesy, because I wonder if he's right. I wonder more if I'll become as jaded when I've been in the war as long as he has. *Like I'm going to live that long.* That seems funny to me. So I laugh, echoing Brice.

The humor of it is contagious, and Brice joins back in. "I think you're wired like me. When the metal is in the air, and the Troglodytes are coming to kill you, you keep a level head, and you don't dwell on the death. You're not squeamish when the blood is boiling off in the vacuum. You're a natural. My advice, don't let your head get in the way too much. Right now, you react well, with good instincts. Unfortunately, one thing you need to accept from the get-go, everybody dies. They were dead the moment they put on that shitty orange suit. That will be the truth, until we run out of people on earth or we kill every damn last one of these apes and all their little gray popsicle-dick bosses. You and me, we'll die along the way. Accept that, and you'll be fine. We knocked out four Trog ships today, and for a moment, we'd conquered a Trog base. Yet there are nearly a thousand Trogs running around this rock looking for us, and another ten thousand up on that ship. I'd be surprised if we don't die fighting in these caves today. Too bad we don't have one of those MSS propaganda crews on hand to record it all. At least we'd be heroes back on earth."

Chapter 13

My d-pad signals something incoming. I tap it, open the message, click the attachment, and see it's a map.

Blair's on the comm. "We're in Tarlow's control room."

I inform Brice.

He smiles. "Now you know how long we wait, if you're still interested in the answer."

"Tarlow just sent you a map," says Blair.

"I got it," I tell her, "but it looks like only one level."

"He's sending maps of the others."

My d-pad chimes, and I download each image. Not exactly the 3-D interactive, full-color, hologram style I was hoping for. Then again, I wasn't expecting to actually get the maps, either.

"Each level is different," says Tarlow over the comm. "Slightly in some cases, a lot in others, depending on how deep you are. You'll have to open the map for whichever level you find yourself on. Right now you're on sublevel one. The first image I sent."

"Got it," I tell him. "Blair, what's the story with the cameras? There's nobody at this airlock."

"Checking now," she answers with no hint at the friction between us.

That worries me.

She replies, "Tarlow says there are nearly three hundred cameras mounted around the complex. Nearly half are functioning. To make matters worse, there are only six monitors down here, and it's a pain to scroll through."

"Let me control it," says Tarlow, apparently trying to push one of the troops off the computer. "You'll break it."

"Sounds like fun," I tell her. "We'll wait here until you give us an airlock to head to." Better than wandering around and praying. "How many lead to the surface?"

"Seventeen," she answers.

I tell Brice.

To Blair, I say, "Try and keep an eye out for the Trogs coming our way, if you don't mind."

"Working on—" she stops.

"What?" Something is wrong. It's an easy guess.

Brice notices the look on my face. He's patient. He doesn't press. He raises his weapon to his shoulder and points it in one direction down the corridor, and then the other.

"Trogs, coming your way," says Blair, urgently.

The light above the airlock door at the end of the short hall flashes red.

Brice sees it and steps into the main corridor. He wants to use the wall as cover from any fire that might come from that direction.

Eyes still on the airlock door, expecting Trogs to come out, I step around the corner.

Before I can tell Brice it's Trogs, not troops, in the airlock, Brice's railgun bursts a fast series of dull pops—high-velocity rounds tearing through the air.

The sound startles me. They don't make any sound in the vacuum we've been fighting in.

"Trogs!" Brice shouts. "Down the corridor!"

"Blair!" I call. "Who's in the airlock?"

"Trogs. I told you."

Shit.

She doesn't even know about the ones in the main corridor.

I flip my weapon to full auto and leap across the corridor so I can see down to the end without Brice in the way. Even as I'm trying to make out my targets in the distance, I pull the trigger.

The hall fills with tracer-like streaks. Air sizzles and pops. Rounds hit the rock walls and explode in shards of sharp stone.

"What's happening?" Blair asks, as she starts shouting orders to Tarlow.

I can't make out how many Trogs are down there. I see bodies falling, and others jumping into side passages or through doorways. Some are turning their backs and running, exposing their vulnerable side.

"Make 'em pay," Brice tells me.

"How many do you see?" I pull the trigger, noticing most of Brice's shots are hitting the walls up and down the hall. "Dammit, you're wasting ammo! What's wrong?"

"Not wasting!" he shouts.

Shots are coming back at us—I can't see the shooters through all the dust and debris blown off the wall.

And they can't see me!

Then I understand. Brice created a smokescreen for us.

"Kane! Kane!" Blair's worried, but I'm kinda busy.

I pull back into the side hall, take out one of my two remaining C4 blocks and stick it to the wall at shoulder height next to a sign that indicates the cafeteria is to the left.

"Time to go!" shouts Brice.

"One sec."

He glances over, clearly irritated, then sees what I'm doing. "Hurry."

I take a quick look at the airlock door. The light flashes yellow. Using my d-pad, I set the charge for a timed detonation of forty seconds, enough time for the Trogs to come out of the airlock, head toward the main hall, and pause as they figure out something is going on.

God, I hope the timing works out.

"Ready!"

Brice glances at me, turns, and runs.

I max my defensive grav and follow him at full speed in the direction of the cafeteria.

Chapter 14

"Blair," I shout as I run, "if Tarlow has cameras in this part of sub one, we could use some intel."

Brice rounds a corner, sliding as he goes, and hits the wall.

Right behind him and running just as fast, I hit the wall, too. My defensive grav bounces me down to the floor and then up off the opposite wall.

"Turn that shit down," Brice yells as he runs on ahead.

I'm spinning head over heels, and it takes a moment to get my feet back under me.

Brice is well ahead by the time I'm running again.

I crank down my defensive grav though I'm agonizing over whether it's the right thing to do. The field probably already saved me from a shot in the back. Brice is twenty meters ahead now, and the chasing Trogs are twenty meters closer.

An explosion thunders and a shockwave hits me, knocking me down face-first. The grav bounces me right back up, and I impact the wall again.

"Goddammit!" I adjust the deflective grav even further, find my feet, lose some time to the pursuing Trogs, and start running again. I don't see Brice. The passage is empty ahead of me. I hit the comm. "Brice, can you hear me?" No immediate response. "Blair, where'd Brice go?"

"We're trying," she calls, caught up in the excitement as if she were in the hall with us. "I had a camera. Two of them in the main corridor, and they just went black."

Ahead, far down the hall, I see a helmet poke out of a doorway. I skid to a halt as I bring my rifle up.

"It's me!" Brice shouts, raising a palm. Now that we're in line-of-sight, his signal reaches me again.

I lower my railgun and run.

"Where are you?" Blair asks. "All I see are dead Trogs and debris in the air."

"Off the main corridor," I pant. "Last sign I saw said 'cafeteria this way'."

I hear Tarlow rattling off something as he works. "There!"

"Got you," Blair tells me, suddenly calm.

Brice ducks in through the doorway and I see there's a sign attached to the wall by the door.

"Definitely the cafeteria," I tell Blair. "We're going in. Please tell me there's a back way out."

"Yes, yes!" Tarlow shouts at me. "The other side of the cafeteria exits to a parallel hall, and through the back of the kitchen there's a doorway leading to a service lift."

"Trogs?" I ask. I already know there aren't any inside, or Brice wouldn't have waved me to follow. "Which way to safety?"

"Looking," Blair tells me, and then to Tarlow she yells, "You need to be faster at changing cameras."

"I'm going as fast as I can, you hemorrhoidal shrew!" Apparently, Tarlow has a short fuse. "This system… it's just pieces, scraps."

Good God, I was hoping for a tactical advantage with the cameras, and all I'm seeing is another layer of clusterfuck. I hit the double swinging doors, and I'm in the cafeteria. The bulbs in the ceiling are burning daylight bright. I spot Brice across the basketball court-sized space, fingering a control panel on the wall.

He glances back and me and jogs my way. "How close are they?

I'm out of breath and adrenaline is beating me up from the inside. "I didn't look."

"Well, dammit, do!"

I unfreeze my feet, step back to the door, and peek out. Down at the turn in the hall, a few Trogs are tentatively coming around the corner, scanning the walls for booby traps.

"At the corner." I smile wickedly, because I know my bomb did more than kill some. "Slow. They're expecting another trap."

Brice laughs, "That was good thinking, fast thinking, planting that charge. How many are left?"

"Blair," I call, "I need a Trog count. How many are out there?"

"The hall on the other side of the cafeteria is clear." Blair is rattling out the words fast and accurate. "The camera in the service lift is out. In the hall you and Brice used to access the cafeteria, the camera is mounted down at the end. I can see what you saw when you peeked out a second ago, only my view is worse."

"How many are coming?" I ask.

"Maybe ten so far. Fifteen now."

"Fifteen *plus*," I tell Brice.

He's kicking chairs, and realizes almost immediately their magnetized feet are holding them to the floor. He starts jerking them up and setting them adrift in the light-g. "Three days?" he asks. "They'll hang in the air for three days?"

I shrug and nod. I don't understand what he's doing. "Something like that."

"Help me, man."

I reach for the nearest chair, three or four meters inside the door.

"Not that one."

It's alone, just sitting there. "What?"

"All that bouncing off the walls rattled your brains, Kane. Take a deep breath, get in the game. I set a charge under that one."

Duh!

"Leave some of the other chairs on the floor, so they don't seem out of place. The rest in the air."

I run through the cafeteria, picking up tables and chairs, sending them off in different directions. It's 3D billiards with utilitarian furniture.

"Blair," I call, "I need a status."

"Maybe twenty in the hall," she tells me. "Pretty brave. Walking fast. You've got maybe thirty seconds. What the hell are you doing in the cafeteria?"

"Thirty seconds," I tell Brice.

He points to the door across the room, the one exiting to the other hallway. "Move over there. Stand in the open doors. Wait for the Trogs to come through. Make sure they see. Shoot a few if you have to, but miss. Then duck."

"Where are you—"

"Do it," he tells me. "Wait for the blast, then hurry your ass back in here and be ready to shoot. Oh, and max your deflective grav once you're in the hall, just in case. Don't forget to jack it back down before you return."

I'm thinking that'll be the best time to have it maxed—well maybe the second-best. I see his point. Poor suit control isn't worth the added defense. He's lived through two years of this war. I've barely lived through two days. I need to listen to him. I run to the far doors.

Chapter 15

I pull both doors open and push the handles into magnet catches on the walls to keep them there. I peek into the narrow corridor, just in case. It's empty. All the Trogs are in the other hall.

"Don't trust me?" Blair asks, actual humor in her voice, except definitely no laugh.

"Of course I do." Empty words, but my adrenaline is still coursing, my brain is on full alert, multi-tasking my way through everything now, max computational speed. For an organic brain anyway.

I turn back toward the cafeteria.

Where the hell did Brice go?

"In the kitchen," he comms. "Behind the buffet counter."

In hushed tones, Blair tells me, "The Trogs will be at the door on the other side of the cafeteria in a moment."

I don't say anything about the unnecessary whisper. All of us humans suffer from our upbringing. "How many?"

"Just the twenty-five or so."

Just.

I laugh. Oh, why the hell not?

I step into the corridor and put my back to a wall beside the open door. The Trogs coming into the cafeteria won't be able to see me.

"What are you doing?" Brice is pissed.

"This'll work better," I say. "Trust me."

"Yes, Major."

I'm guessing that'll be the way he addresses me from now on when he's not happy. If we live through this. "Blair, tell me when they're inside."

"Looking through the doors now," she tells me. "They're confused about the floating chairs. They're conferring in the hall."

Waiting.

"They've pulled the doors open," she says. "Several are looking inside again."

That'll have to be my cue.

I jump across the open doorway like I was running up the corridor and stop as if I'm surprised to see the Trogs across the cafeteria. I bring my railgun to my hip and fire a spray of slugs into the wall above their heads as I fake a stumble and fall out of their view.

At least that's what they see.

Once out of sight, I throw my back against the wall and raise my rifle, ready to ambush any Trogs who come through. "Brice! Brice! They're yours."

I hear his voice, but there's too much static to understand.

"They're all coming inside now," says Blair. "Not running. Not hurrying. No, not all. Half of them. Most of them."

Thunder rocks sublevel one. The air feels like it's exploding again. I'm knocked over on my side as pieces of furniture and bodies fly through the doors I'd propped open.

"Lost my cafeteria cam!" shouts Blair.

Doesn't matter. Not to me. Not right this second. I have my assignment. I reduce my defensive grav as I jump back up and plant myself at the corner. I peek inside. Magically clear.

Well, not magic, chemistry and physics did their work. The blast blew everything away from the center of the room.

Much of the furniture and Trog debris is either stuck to or bouncing back off the walls.

Some of the Trogs are moving fast, rebounding on too much defensive grav, beach balls with no control, arms and legs swinging, alive but dazed. Others are shooting through the room, balloons rocketing red plumes of blood vapor, parts of furniture lethally protruding from their bodies.

I shout, "Blair, did we get them all?"

"No!" she warns. "Seven or eight are still in the other hall. They're coming!"

I look to the other side of the cafeteria just in time to see them crowding through the door.

I drop to a knee and fire.

The Trogs are ready for my assault with chest plates set to max deflect. My rounds arc into the floor, walls, and ceiling.

They're coming quick, not full-speed, but fast enough to make me plan my retreat. The Trogs seem to understand that the grav from their frontal plates is more effective when combined, when they're packed tightly together.

"Goddamn!" I shout. "These things aren't supposed to be smart."

"Don't believe everything you see on TV," Brice tells me. "Don't get up and run, Kane. Draw them closer."

I know what he has in mind, but it's *my* life he's gambling with.

I scoot back, just a bit, enough to let the Trogs know I'm scared. I flip from auto back to single-shot. No sense wasting ammo.

They've crossed half the cafeteria, and they're picking up speed as their confidence builds. They know they have me.

Fortunately, not all things we know as fact turn out to be true.

A stream of hypervelocity slugs traces out from the far corner of the cafeteria, raking across the Trogs' exposed backs.

Blood sprays into the air. Limbs fly away. Torsos rip. Troglodytes fall.

Seemingly, before the slugs have all found their marks, Brice is on his feet, stalking through the chaotic space, tapping out the remaining Trogs who aren't dead yet.

"What's happening?" Blair asks. "What's going on? Did it work?"

"Clear," I tell her. "We're both good."

Brice moves toward me, a grim smile on his face.

I give him a nod.

He nods back. No, 'Yes, Major' bullshit.

We're comrades again.

And fuck, we're good at this shit.

CHAPTER 16

Blair is shouting, "Kane! Kane!"

A distant explosion rumbles through the stone in the walls. There's another fight somewhere. I hope our troops are getting the best of it.

I look around as Brice and I run through a passageway, not going anywhere in particular, just getting away from the scene of noisy mayhem we just sewed. More Trogs are sure to be on their way to investigate.

"Kane!"

"Yeah?" I pant. "Are we back in trouble?"

"I don't know where you are."

That explains her yelling. She felt like she was losing control.

"Stop for a sec," I tell Brice, as I look around for pursuers.

Brice is uncomfortable. We're midway between two intersections, easy targets for Trogs coming from either end. He points to a cross hall ahead. "We'll stop up there."

He's already running.

"We're looking for you." Blair's voice sounds anxious through the crackle on the comm.

"Here," says Tarlow. "I think they went this way."

At the intersection, Brice peeks around the corners, readies his weapon, and says, "Okay."

I come to a stop beside him and glance at the signs on the wall. I comm Blair, "Intersection of halls Q and J. There's an airlock door to a machine shop or something just down from us. Can't tell for sure—the sign is all scratched up."

"I know where that is," comms Tarlow.

"Call up the camera," Blair tells him. To me, she says, "We have eleven of our people in a repair hangar that—"

"Ships?" I interrupt, too excited. Hangars imply flight, which means we have a chance to rocket the hell out of here. "Are there ships in there?"

"Not really," she counters, seeming to take some satisfaction from correcting me. "Big pieces of equipment. Mining…things. It's a huge place, open to the vacuum. There's an airlock they can use to access sub one."

Probably no ships, but survivors of the bombardment. I nudge Brice and smile. Good news coming over the comm. I ask Blair, "How do I get there?"

"Ask her about the Trogs." Brice has his priorities in order. "Where are they?"

"Most of them are on the surface," Tarlow informs us.

"Most?" Derision wrapped up in a one-syllable question. We have no room for ambiguity.

Tarlow hears every drip of meaning in my response. "Don't get your knickers in a knot. I'm trying to help."

"Blair," I ask, "do we know how many Trogs are down here? Do we know where they are?"

"We've spotted two squads," she answers. "Six in one, a dozen in the other. The six are in the cafeteria. They went in a few minutes ago, but now I can't see them. The cameras in that room aren't working, so we don't know what they're doing."

Like I give a shit what they're up to inside. I don't say that, of course. "Let me know if they come this way. The other squad?"

"Headed in your direction," she tells me. "They're cautious. They have a ghost Trog leading them. He seems smart. Checking rooms as they go, methodically and slowly. As long as you don't make any noise and stay away from them, you don't have to worry."

I ask again. "Where are they?"

"Near the corner of Oscar and Frieda One," Tarlow explains.

"Oscar and Frieda?" I roll my eyes and Brice sees. "Fucking hallway names." Back to Tarlow, I ask, "You mean halls O and F?"

"It's what they call them up here." Tarlow is defensive again. "I don't—"

"Look," I cut him off. "Nobody's blaming you. We're just trying to live through this. The signs are labeled in letters. Talk to me in letters. I don't have time to learn your naming system." I'm scrolling around on the map image on my d-pad, trying to find the intersection where we're standing.

Brice leans over for a peek. He points. "Is that the cafeteria there?"

I stop scrolling for a moment. "Yeah."

He looks back up the corridor.

A quick series of explosions shakes the walls.

"Is that coming from down there?" I ask over the comm.

"On the surface?" replies Tarlow.

"Railguns or C4?" I hope the bombardment hasn't restarted.

"Can't say." Tarlow sounds sheepish. "No camera up there can see through the dust."

I put the explosions out of my mind. We took several turns and ran down through a few long passages to get here. I glance around. "We're safe for the moment." Then back to Blair. "That group is still in the cafeteria, right?"

"Right."

I finally find O and F on the map. "Here," I tell Brice as I point. "A dozen here with a Ghost Trog in the lead. They're searching for us room by room." I scroll the map to our position. "This is where we are. I think."

"I've found you on camera," says Blair.

"I feel all warm and fuzzy." It's a dickish response, but the least offensive of the two I was contemplating. "Where do we need to go?"

"Airlock thirteen," Tarlow instructs. "Thirteen."

I'm scrolling my map image again, looking for the number. "I only see hallway labels."

"The image doesn't have any airlock numbers on it?"

I locate what looks like the airlock we entered the subterranean level through. "Doesn't look like it to me."

"I must have sent you the wrong file."

Brice isn't hearing Tarlow and Blair, but my side of it is telling him enough. "Cluster?"

I nod.

"Thirteen is at the end of Oscar One."

"Oscar One?" I make it sound like an insult. "The hallway the ghost Trog and his squad are in, that's Oscar One?"

"Yes," answers Tarlow like he doesn't understand the connection.

"It sounds bad," Blair tells us, I guess trying to offer comfort with her bureaucratic coldness. "I think we can pull it off. There's a cross hall, Einstein One," she pauses and corrects herself, "E-1. If you can get there, it intersects with O near the airlock."

"How near?" I ask.

"Near enough."

That's a lie. I have no doubt. "Which way do we need to go?"

Chapter 17

I peek around the corner. O-1 is wide, maybe four meters, one of the main corridors on this level, running three hundred meters across the complex. Way down at the far end, I think I see a green light above an airlock door. Just over halfway, Trogs are in the hall, some are loitering. Others are filing into a room through its double airlock doors. Nearly every room on this level has an airlock in case of a depressurization accident somewhere else on the base.

On the comm link with Brice, I share a realization, "This place is huge."

"Nine levels, the size of this maze," Brice leans for a quick look around the corner, "I'd say you're right."

"It must have been a profitable venture before it turned to the rebel cause and became a Free Army base."

"Probably still is," suggests Brice. "Unless the Free Army built it out this way."

Recalling the wide variety of shops and storage rooms we passed as we were finding our way here, I deduce, "There's a lot of infrastructure here. Seems like overkill for a few hundred people running an ice mining operation."

Brice peeks down the hall at the Trogs again, then takes a look in the other direction. "What do you think? Thirty meters of straight hall with not an iota of cover between here and the door?"

The door at this end of the corridor is the one we're supposed to bring our eleven soldiers through. I look at a thirty-meter kill zone—one that over Blair's camera looked 'close enough.' I sigh. "This blows."

"Before you give yourself an aneurism," says Brice. "Is this the right airlock?"

"Not that it matters much." I point a thumb in the other direction. "The Trogs are about halfway up the hall. The same distance from each airlock."

"Check with Blair."

I comm her and Tarlow in. "Are we at the right end of O-1?"

"Yes, the airlock should be just to your right," answers Tarlow.

"Just?"

Brice hears my side of the conversation again, and his dark laugh suggests maybe he's thinking of heading down to level three and punching his fist through Tarlow's faceplate.

I say to them, "I'm hoping while we were on the way over here you came up with a plan to make this work. Do you know how long we'll be exposed out there? The Trogs will see us. I'd prefer not to be shot making this happen."

"Don't get whiney on me now." Blair's mean inner core is shining through.

"I'm just saying, if the plan is to shoot it out in front of the airlock, then me and Brice are ditching it. We'll find another route through this maze so we can flank those Trogs and ambush them when they're coming out of a room. We can deal with getting our troops inside later."

"There's no later," Blair triumphantly tells me. "One of the troops up top found the airlock door, and they're divvying up in groups to come through."

"Great." I check my ammo, and heave a weary sigh.

"It's not as bad as you think," Tarlow offers. "I've tapped into the lighting control systems on sub one."

"The whole floor?" I ask, perking up.

"Yes. Give it about thirty seconds."

"Give what?"

Red and white emergency lights start flashing down the hall, casting splashes of color in our direction.

Brice looks at me with a question on his face.

I shrug, and peek around the corner. "I think this is Tarlow's doing."

The lights in the hundred meters of hall closest to our airlock turn off.

Those flashing are down at the other end.

Trogs down that way have their weapons up, and they're looking around, confused.

"This is it," says Blair. "It's what we can do."

Brice looks me up and down.

I glance down to check my color. In some places, my worn orange suits shows through. Mostly I'm still coated in asteroid dust.

"We'll look like shadows against these stone walls," says Brice. "Pretty good camouflage for this environment. With the light show, I think we're safe to go." He doesn't wait for me to agree. He jogs into the hall and heads for the airlock door.

I follow, casting worried glances back down toward the Trogs.

Near them, lights are shining brightly down from the ceiling. With me and Brice in darkness, I'm hoping they can't see us.

Ahead of me, Brice hits the airlock door release and it immediately swings open. The interior light blinks on as he jumps inside and it bathes him in a bright white. The same glow silhouettes me.

"Shit!" The words escape even as I'm diving inside to hide behind a bulkhead and press myself against an interior wall.

"The lights in the airlock, Tarlow! Kill the lights in the airlock!"

Blair spews a fast tirade at him.

"I, I… they weren't reading on, when I started," babbles Tarlow.

Brice punches the button to swing the airlock door shut.

"I would have…" Tarlow's words get lost in Blair's ridicule.

The door, slowly, way too slowly, comes to a close.

The comm line goes silent for several painfully slow seconds, and then Blair passes us the news. "They're coming your way."

"Disappointing." It seems like a good time to switch from sarcasm to understatement, a subtle form of sarcasm, in truth.

Turning anxiously to Brice, I ask, "How long did it take for the airlock to cycle last time?" I don't ask 'how long before the Trogs get here?' 'What do you think they'll do when they run up and peek through the small glass viewport in the door and see two humans inside?' 'Will they shoot through the door?' 'Will those disruptor blades cut steel?' All valid questions.

Air is hissing out of the airlock.

The sound is changing with the lowering pressure.

Brice is patient and prepared. His back is against the opposite door, and his rifle is ready.

"Four," says Blair. "The rest are staying behind. Four are coming to investigate?"

"Running?" I ask.

"Jogging," she tells me. "Not fast. Cautious."

The air inside is almost gone.

Just a few more seconds.

Brice takes a glance through the exterior glass.

"What do you see?" I ask him.

"Stairs," he answers. "Dust. Not as thick as outside, but it's pretty murky out there.

A light above the exterior door flashes to green.

Brice pops the door open, and I nearly bowl him over to get through.

In a rush, we push the door closed behind us.

The light inside goes out.

"Made it," I comm Blair, as Brice mounts the stairs.

He's calling to the troops in the hanger. The metallic ore in the dust is crackling the link with static, but I hear other voices.

"Don't shoot," Brice orders. "We're coming up."

"Contact," I tell Blair. "Keep me posted on those Trogs. Also, we'll need directions to another airlock so we can come back inside."

Chapter 18

Blair tells me. "One of the Trogs hit the button to cycle the airlock."

"Brice," I call as I reach the top of the stairs beside him. We're at ground level. "Four Trogs will be in the airlock in a minute."

He looks down into the stairwell, twenty steps deep with the airlock exit at the end. His grim smile tells me all I need to know. Best odds we've had all day.

Dust hanging in the vacuum casts a ghostly gray over a digging machine as big as a bus, roughly stacked parts for a disassembled conveyor, drilling rigs of various sizes, a grav lift, and several oddly configured spaceships. I can make out the webbing of metal joists spanning a ceiling nearly lost in the haze above us. Several large holes are cut through the roof, each looking large enough to fly a small ship through. The hangar's walls are far enough away from us to be obscured by the dust.

"At least this gray crap isn't as thick in here as it was outside," I mutter.

Human figures solidify out of the haze and come toward us.

"We have thirty seconds to set up an ambush," Brice tells them as he nods his head down the stairs. "Four Trogs will be cycling out. They're following us." He starts to point at soldiers, directing them where to go. "We want the Trogs well away from the airlock stairs before we pull the triggers. I don't want one getting back down and punching the button. If that happens, and one gets in, we'll have another twenty coming to the party. And that's just from the inside. There are more out there. The faster we kill these, the more likely our presence here will remain a secret."

"We know," says one of the soldiers, a sergeant Kendrick. It's clear she's put herself in charge of the unit, though I can't tell whether the rest of the grunts are from one platoon or several.

Turns out, it doesn't matter.

Brice and Kendrick quickly divide the soldiers into crossfire positions, leaving each one kneeling or standing behind a piece of metal equipment for cover.

I find myself beside Brice, pointing my rifle over the top of a small survey car parked directly above the airlock chamber in the ground below. When the Trogs come out, they'll be walking up the stairs with their backs to us.

Brice points at the dust in the stairwell as he nudges me with his elbow. "Watch the light reflecting on that gray shit. When it changes color, they'll be coming."

Good warning system, I think.

A moment later, the hue reflected from the dust particles switches from green to white.

Brice warns everyone.

"All four are exiting the airlock," Blair confirms over my comm.

Thirteen of us are arrayed to fire. Half behind, half from their right flank.

They don't need my rifle, and they don't need my full attention. The Trogs won't last two seconds after Brice gives the word to fire. I kill my outbound comm to the platoon so my voice won't distract them. "Blair, any word on other survivors?"

"We have three at airlock twelve," she tells me. "Maybe five or so in a tunnel coming from one of the Trog's gun pits."

"You're not sure on the count?" I ask.

"No cameras that way," says Tarlow, making sure we all know it's not his fault. "The airlock they came through was in the gun pit the Trogs constructed in the center of the colony. We caught a glimpse of them by sheer luck from a camera down a passageway they crossed in front of."

"Where are they headed?"

"I'm leading them with the lights." Tarlow is proud of the solution. "I'm darkening the halls they should avoid, and lighting the ones I want them to take."

"Are they?" I ask. "Following?"

"They're wary," answers Blair, "but they're taking direction, so far."

A Trog is looking out of the stairwell thirty feet in front of my position, scanning for human forms, looking for movement, just like any good soldier would.

Another Trog comes up beside him.

They're not in a hurry.

One points a finger at something it deems significant.

"Everyone wait," Brice declares. "This will be easy if we snap the trap at the right time."

"Where's the nearest airlock to us," I ask Blair, "if we go over the surface?"

"Far," answers Tarlow. "At least a hundred meters and there's no straight-line path."

Straight line? What the hell does that matter? Nobody can walk a straight line out there. "Landmarks along the way?" I ask. "Buildings, communication dishes, anything?

"Yes, a building in your way," answers Tarlow. "I need to call up the surface map to provide you the shape."

Ugh.

The first two Trogs are on the ground ten paces from the stairs, waiting, looking for danger. Two take the final steps to the surface in unison and crouch.

They're hunting, a behavior I've not seen from them yet. At least not from their low-level grunts.

One of the two Trogs behind turns to scan the area around the stairwell, the area where I'm hiding with Brice.

"Trogs don't usually do that," Brice tells me to confirm my observations. "The way they fight, in massive formations and frontal charges, they're not used to having to worry about flanking attacks."

I barely nod. I don't want to give away our position.

The boldest one, the leader, moves forward. He has one of their single-shot rifles. The other three are carrying disruptors.

They're all well away from the stairwell, moving cautiously toward a pathway past the bus-size digger.

"Fire!" Brice orders.

A glowing gridwork of railgun slugs tears through the dingy slurry, leaving trails devoid of dust particles, and etching bright lines on my retinas. Many of the trails bend as they encounter the Trog's defensive fields. Most of the shots from behind burn straight through their backs, some punching holes, others fragmenting inside and shredding flesh in chunks huge enough to tear away arms and legs.

They look like marionettes, disintegrating and jerking, directionless and gory as the micro-g tugs gently to pull them down.

I guess instantly they're all dead, but they don't fall.

"Cease fire," orders Brice.

A Trog spasms.

Three more rounds rip through its back. It stops moving.

The bodies drift in clouds of dust that swirl with their passing.

Blood sprays from suit tears, mingling with the gray, turning it red.

A string of intestine swirls out of a Trog's shredded torso, hosing its digestive liquids into the evaporating vacuum.

"They're all coming." Blair is disappointed but not alarmed.

All?

"The ghost Trog?" I ask. "And his squad."

"The ones from the cafeteria, too," she answers. "They're not wasting any time."

I convey the information to Brice.

"Everybody, hold your positions." He points to several soldiers. "Move those bodies out of sight. Do it quick."

Four grunts jump up, hustling like real-live soldiers.

Over the comm, I ask, "Blair, how close?"

"They'll be outside the airlock in twenty seconds."

The bodies are easy to move in the low g, easy to hide. The haze of blood, and the red-stained dust, isn't going anywhere. It'll be readily seen by any wary Trog coming up the airlock stairs.

I nudge Brice. "What do you think?"

"We need to be ready just in case, but this won't work twice," he tells me. "Telepathy and all. If those downstairs are coming this way, it's because they know something happened up here. It's exactly why ambush doesn't work on Trogs."

"What do you mean?" I ask. "It's been working all day."

"Trogs have all got the bug in their heads."

"I thought they were naturally telepathic?" I realize immediately I'm repeating crap I learned from MSS newsfeeds.

Damn! How much of the shit I've always accepted as true comes from them?

I know lots of things. I don't tend to remember where I learned each bit of information. That's going to be a problem.

"Next time you have a chance to look inside one's skull," says Brice—*because in war, that's the kind of thing that could come up any day*—"look for the spaghetti bug. Just like the pictures of the ones you see back on earth. A Trog brain looks like a human one. Their skull bones are exactly like ours, only thicker, more bulbous. I always wondered about that, the similarities. Makes sense, I guess. Now that we know Grays are running the Trog show, too."

That's all interesting stuff, but it's not what I'm asking. "What do you mean about the ambushes working and not working?"

"These Trogs have some kind of militaristic culture," says Brice. "At least it looks that way to me, but hey, I've only seen their armies. It skews my perceptions. Know what I mean?"

I do. I nod.

"I think they've warred with each other in the past, maybe they still do," he muses. "Who knows? The universe is a big place. The thing that won't work if they're all telepathic, is ambush. They'd never walk into one when fighting other Trogs because they'd always sense the Trogs hiding to shoot them in the back. Now, coming to fight us, ambush isn't a tactic they know exists, so they walk right into the traps when we set them."

"But," I add, because I know that's what's coming next.

"But," he continues, "not all of these Trogs died instantly when we shot them. However Trogs do it, one of them let his buddies downstairs in on our secret. Maybe not the details, but enough to let the others know if they come charging up here, we'll fuck 'em up.

I'm trying to reconcile this with the behavior of the Trogs in that line I killed when Blair and I were following those nine through the dust storm earlier. I wonder, did the instant death simply end communication? No SOS went out?

"If other Trogs are close enough," Brice deduces, "the ones up here on the surface will be closing in to kill us while we're waiting to spring an ambush that will never happen."

"We can't stay," I realize. It's the logical conclusion.

Blair chimes in. "Kane, you need to know, you've got about twenty Trogs down in the tunnel outside the airlock, waiting for you to come out. They're setting an ambush."

I look at Brice. "For stupid cavemen, they sure do learn quick."

Chapter 19

"Blair," I ask, "are all of the Trogs on sublevel one in the hall waiting to ambush us when we come out of the airlock?"

"All we know of," she replies, clearly wondering what I'm getting at.

"That's not the answer I want." I'm slipping into the realm of unrealistic expectations. I know half the cameras in the complex don't function. "Kick Tarlow in the nuts if you have to. I need a one-hundred-percent accurate answer."

"I will, but—"

"No buts. No time," I tell her. "Tarlow, are you on the line? Get me that answer. You've got sixty seconds, maybe less."

Tarlow squeaks a response through a throat clenched in fright.

I'm tempted to add another threat but I know I'm asking for a degree of certainty he probably can't provide. Still, he needs to try.

"What's up?" asks Brice. "What do you have in mind?"

"All the Trogs on sub one are waiting inside to attack us." I glance at the soldiers around us. "As long as they stay there, all of the other airlocks are open. All of sublevel one is safe."

Blair reaches the same conclusion, and immediately sees the pitfall. "With no lucky run-in with Tarlow, they'll be lost once they're inside. With the limited number of monitors we have down here, we can't use the hallway lights to lead them."

I comm to Brice. "You still have the network access code?" I'm working the next steps in the problem.

He nods. "The Brice-meister doesn't delete important information."

Brice-meister?

Sometimes he's a very odd man. I tell him, "Share it with Sergeant Kendrick and the others." Switching back to Blair, I tell her, "I don't know yet how many of these eleven will be able to set up their d-pads to communicate on the base network—some of them, no doubt. As soon as they're on, provide them with surface and sublevel maps. Blair, you and Tarlow need to guide them to the nearest airlock and then disperse them on sub one so they can reach all the inner airlocks quickly and intercept survivors who make it through. Make sure they stay away from the Trogs outside the airlock below. Rally them all down on sublevel three where your team is holed up."

Blair huffs.

I realize I've dumped too many imperatives on her and offended her sense of in-charge-liness.

"They won't fit in here," insists Tarlow.

"If you're talking," I tell him, "it better be because you're done with your survey of sub one. Is sub one clear?"

No answer.

"Blair," I catch myself before I proceed. I need to ask, or she and I are going to descend into another useless argument. "I don't know how to deal with Tarlow's concern about the size of his hidey-hole. Is this something you can resolve?" Jesus, the seconds on that long request feel wasted.

"I'll take care of things down here?" she declares. "What's your plan up there?"

Looking at Brice, hoping he agrees to stick with me, I say, "I'm staying in the hangar outside the airlock. As long as we're present here keeping the attention of the Trogs below, they'll continue to wait. Sub one will stay clear." That's a logical leap based on a guess and a handful of static dependencies changing with each passing second.

"Keeping their attention?" Brice laughs grimly.

"You in?" I ask him.

"Somebody once told me I was fucking good at this shit." His quick nod follows. He's in. No doubt.

"Find us some volunteers to stay," I tell him.

"Volunteers?" he asks.

"Gotta be." I look at him with the seriousness of the degrading situation clearly visible on my face. Hundreds of Trogs will be closing in on us through the slurry of dust and rock outside. The situation could be deadly for those who remain.

At least the ones who make their way down to hook up with Blair will have a chance. They can fight in the tunnels if Blair can find a competent tactician hidden inside her dunghill of self-importance. Or they can surrender and ride a slave ship back to Troglandia—or whatever the hell the Trogs call their home planet—to spend the rest of their natural lives studding out generations of serfs for the Grays there.

Better than dying, I guess.

Well, not if it were me. I'll die before I kneel again.

Brice is talking to the troops. Passing out the info. Finding the volunteers.

"Tarlow." I have no more patience and no more time. "Give me that answer.

"Clear," he tells me.

"You'll bet your life on it?" That's what I'll be doing, and what I'll be asking my grunts to do.

He gulps audibly. "I can't say more Trogs won't come and—"

"I'm not asking you to predict the future," I hiss. "My people need to reach your location safely. Make your shitty surveillance system do its job and make this happen."

"I think you've got his attention," says Blair. "You do what you need to do. We'll do our part."

"Good luck," I tell her. It comes out harsh, but it's sincere.

"Good luck to you, too, Kane." She starts to say something else, pauses, and fumbles through a few starts. Nothing else comes over the comm.

"Don't you worry about us," I tell them, as I glance at Brice. Three soldiers are with him. The rest are heading toward the far end of the hangar. "People coming your way."

Chapter 20

Do-nothing time starts in earnest.

The twenty-two Trogs inside the airlock stay where they are, waiting us out. Of course, if Brice is right, and he likely is, they have another plan in the works.

On our side, eight of our soldiers made for the next closest airlock, leaving three with us. Brice directed the grunts to take up positions watching from the hangar's corners. One corner goes unguarded, leaving us to play the odds.

All told, we have a handful of C4 charges between us. Brice plants them where he believes they'll kill the most Trogs when the attack comes.

We wait.

And wait.

Blair stays in contact.

With all the Trogs on sub one tied down, things settle down in the station's subterranean levels. Survivors of the bombardment trickle in through unguarded airlocks.

I listen at quarter-volume while Blair organizes and directs them safely down to sublevel three.

Both sides in our asteroid battle are moving their pieces around the board, preparing.

Becoming bored with the wait, yet feeling some optimism at our progress, I say to Brice, "If this keeps up for another—I don't know, twenty or thirty minutes—we can bail out of this hangar, find a nearby airlock and head downstairs. We might avoid a fight for now."

"No."

No? That's it? One syllable.

"Why do you say that?"

He takes his eyes off our surroundings and settles them on me long enough for me to understand that my question was stupid.

"Seriously, why?" I peer into the dusty shadows, looking for movement as I start imagining every puff of cloud is a Trog materializing out of the dark.

"Because The Brice is right," he tells me. "I'm in constant contact with our lookouts. Nobody's in here but us."

I point to the corner of the building where I know no guard is watching. I know with the debris in the air as thick as it is outside, no one on any corner of the hangar can see down to another corner. "We're vulnerable, from that direction."

Brice shakes his head. "You're thinking like a human."

"How's that?"

"Bugs in their heads," He taps the side of his helmet. "Deadly if you forget it."

"Help me with the logic here."

"It's telepathy," says Brice, "like we talked about. Same reason ambush doesn't work. Sneaky stealth is pointless. You can't surprise an enemy you can't hide from. Battlefield tactics are a waste of time. You can't outmaneuver an enemy who reads your plans right out of your own mind. There's no chess aspect to their war. For them, it comes down to a simple thing—one-on-one, warrior domination."

I don't admit it, but it makes perfect sense.

"I think they've got a big macho culture about it," says Brice, "which is why they prefer the disruptor blades over the railguns. Maybe it's an honor thing, a way to prove themselves."

"They don't fight us one-on-one," I argue.

"War is still war," he counters. "They need to win, just like we do. Slaughtering your enemies and filling mass graves with their bodies is the best way to do that. Probably the Grays have crammed whatever passes for media in their culture with loads of bullshit about what kind of gnarly little monsters we are. The same as our media tells us about them. It's easy for soldiers to massacre vile beasts. If the Trog grunts believed we were thinking, feeling beings just like them, but prettier, they'd probably feel obligated to fight us one-on-one according to whatever passes for honor among them."

"You've put a lot of thought into this," I observe.

"War is a lot about waiting," he says. "Lots of time to ruminate."

"Do you suppose they're like us—thinking, feeling, with families?"

Brice answers with a shrug, and adds, "War is a like a fire. You light it with some hate, and once your loved ones start dying, emotion fans the flame. It grows until everybody wants to slaughter the monsters killing their friends. Doesn't matter what the enemy looks like, whether they're loving fathers or devoted daughters, priests or artists, saints or sinners, they are all monsters."

"But?" I ask, looking for some hope in what seems to be the story of all humankind, a story with no room for a happy ending.

He shrugs again. "No buts. Just shit the way it is."

Bleak.

Probably true.

Maybe the best we can hope for are respites where we can pretend the current peace will last forever.

We wait in silence, watching the gray slurry drift between machines in various states of repair.

Finally, I ask, "What's going to happen?"

"You should know."

Trying to defer, I say, "You're the experienced one."

"You've got the bug in your head," Brice argues. "It's pretty much the same thing they've got. Can't you sense them? Can't you read their minds?"

I laugh.

"Why's that funny?" He's put off. He thinks I'm holding out on him. "Is there some spaghetti-head secret that I should know?"

I shake my head. "You know, if Phil were here—"

"Phil?" Brice scoffs. Phil has a way of turning people against him, whether acquaintances or those he's known for years.

I tap my head. "The implant, you know, the Grays don't give us an owner's manual with this thing when they put it in. They don't even know how to instruct us in its use. When I was a kid, my teachers all had implants, bugs installed when they were adults." I snort when I think of how ridiculous the whole thing was. "Even as first- and second-graders, having had bugs in our heads since a few weeks after birth, we were doing things our teachers could only wish they had the abilities to do. Didn't matter, though."

"How's that?" asks Brice.

"None of us uses the bug up to its potential, not like in the rumors you hear."

"People say it makes you just like a Gray," says Brice. "You can see gravity, talk telepathically. You stop being a *me* and start being an *us*."

"It's not like that." It's nothing like that for me. "Most of us develop one or two bug-related talents. As for me, I became really good at manipulating the Grays' tech, because all of their control systems use grav switches and organic grav-sensitive circuits. I won most of the games in school where manipulation of the real world was the goal."

"You can just move stuff around?" I can't tell whether Brice is awed or vindicated. "Like telekinesis?"

"No," I answer. "Nothing like that. I can't pick up a rock with my mind. If it's built on Gray technology—grav lifts, these suits, our ships—then yes. They all run on circuits that can be manipulated by grav fields. On the micro level, I can influence a grav field, that's how grav switches work. I guess that's kinda like telekinesis."

"Sounds exactly like it," argues Brice. "They say Grays can do that with anything."

"I've heard that, too, yet I've never seen it for real. So I don't know. On the other hand, if you slap enough grav plates and organic control circuits on something, I can control it, no matter what it is."

Brice turns curious. "Is that what you had in the bug-head school, special toys or something? Balls with grav plates and grav switches built in?"

"Yeah. All kinds of stuff like that."

"Learn something new every day," muses Brice. "What about telepathy? The Trogs use their bugs for that. Why can't you?"

"Probably because I've spent all of my life trying to hide what I'm thinking from the Grays. I repress it."

"Secrets?" asks Brice. "So much masturbating you were embarrassed?

We both laugh.

"Hate," I tell him. "I've always wanted to kill them."

"Don't we all." Brice deduces something. "So that's how it is with you spaghetti-heads, then? You're all so busy trying to hide your contempt for the Grays, the telepathic part of your abilities never fully develops."

"I think you're right," I answer. "Except for Phil."

"Phil?" Brice can't believe it. Doesn't want to.

"Not only can he read grav fields better than anybody I've ever met, he reads other people's thoughts better than anyone."

"Everybody's thoughts?" asks Brice.

I guess maybe Brice has entertained some violent images concerning Phil's corpse. Then, the question makes me wonder. I honestly don't know. "I'm pretty sure just other bug-heads and Grays. Though, not really Grays, they're hard to read. It takes a lot of effort, even for Phil. However, for us other kids in school," I shake my head, "we used to play cards with him, and he always won. Always. You couldn't play chess with him, because he always knew what you were up to."

"Just like the Trogs," says Brice. "When they go to war."

"Yeah."

"What I don't get then," says Brice, "is Phil. Does he like the Grays? Did his telepathic abilities grow because he didn't have anything to hide?"

"I haven't thought about these kinds of questions in a long time," I admit. "I don't know about the development of his powers, but I can tell you for sure, he doesn't like Grays."

"So as obnoxious as he is," this thought saddens Brice, "he's talented."

"That's why I picked him for my crew. That, and he and I have been friends since we started school."

"Well, too bad Phil isn't here now." Brice takes a long scan around us. "He'd probably sense those Trogs out there. He could tell us when they're coming."

I agree. "Getting back to what the Trogs are up to, what should we expect?"

"They're out there concentrating their forces. " Brice points in several directions, like he knows exactly where they are. "It's hard with all the shit in the air. It'll take them a while. When they finally get it together, they'll swarm us in overwhelming numbers, from all directions at once. That's pretty much the tactic."

"If they're coming from all directions, then why guard three? Why not just watch one corner of the hangar?"

"I get things wrong just like anybody else. Why not be careful if you can afford it?"

Chapter 21

Blair raises me on the comm, "Kane, are you there?"

Waiting by the phone. "Yup."

"We have seventeen soldiers down in the control center and—"

"The control center?" It sounds like a pretentious name to me. "Tarlow's closet?"

"No. We moved to the station's main control center?"

I don't know what to say. I think Blair has made a fatal mistake. But it's Blair, so I can't just tell her that bluntly. "Do you think you'll be discovered?"

Blair responds to my hesitation with an explanation instead of anger. "Tarlow says the Trogs never come in here. Radios, computers, video screens, Trogs and Grays don't have this kind of tech. They don't know how to use it, and don't have any interest in learning about it."

I don't agree. My bet is there's an educated class of Trog scientists somewhere that would love to get their big clumsy hands on our technology. Or the Grays truly are running this intra-galactic sideshow—big assumptions on them not having come from too far away. Which means they'll steal for themselves any tech they can develop an understanding of and can use to repress their lessers. Just because the current Gray management of earth doesn't appreciate our electronic toys doesn't mean this new bunch won't see the potential. I sum all that mental jabber up with, "I don't think their disinterest will last."

"It'll last for as long as we need." Blair finds it easy to be certain.

There's no point in arguing. "What level is the command center on?"

"Three," she says, "Same level as Tarlow's closet."

"How are you set for Trogs down there?"

"The sublevels are mostly empty." She sounds like she's distracted by something else. "Eighteen appear to be stationed on sub nine guarding the reservoir pens."

"Where the prisoners are being held?" I confirm.

"Yes," she tells me. "Nearly a hundred Trogs are on sub seven."

"Over hundred down in the sublevels with us?" I was becoming spoiled by numbers that measured only by the dozen. "Is that where the Grays are, down on sub seven?"

"Yes. That's right," Blair confirms. "Tarlow tells me there's a rec room down there with enough sunlamps in the ceiling to make it feel like a Saharan summer, earth g, and a lap pool. If you haven't seen it on the map, it's huge. From the glare on the cameras, it looks like the Grays set the lamps' intensity to match wherever they came from. Bright as hell. They like to bask. You know that, right?"

"That they like to sunbathe?" How could I not know that? On clear days back home, the Gray-stink-twig killing my wife pesters her to take him out on the back porch to lie in the sun. The high elevation and intense sunshine are reasons the Grays chose Breck when they first arrived on earth. "Do they stay in there all the time?"

"Tarlow says they haven't left since they took over the station. They run this place from there."

Still an assumption, a likely assumption, yet maybe I'm being silently argumentative. "And the Trogs who guard them."

"They stay mostly in a lobby area open to the hall with the lights turned dim."

I realize I'm gathering info for an assault my troops will have to make. The Grays are the key to controlling this asteroid. They'll need to die. I suspect the Trogs will fall into disarray with their Gray leadership dead. I'm getting ahead of myself.

"Some," says Blair. "The number varies. They come in and out of the lobby on no particular schedule."

"Ghost Trogs?" I need to know if any are down there. They're the most dangerous kind.

"Six inside," she answers. "They go in with the Grays from time to time. None outside. What are you thinking?"

"Nothing yet." I peer into the hangar's obscuring dust, looking for Trogs. "I'm learning what I can. We're in a waiting game up here. Brice is sure the Trogs are massing for an assault outside. Are the twenty-two still waiting for us inside the airlock?"

"They haven't left."

"So, seventeen." I'm talking about our troops down in the control center. I'd hoped for more.

Blair hears the disappointment in my voice. "Another twenty, at least, are in the halls on their way here. I have a handful in airlock six, and it looks like two more at airlock three."

"Oh, that is good."

"It's better than good."

"How so?"

"The warehouse where the prisoners were held wasn't damaged during the raid."

"How do you know?" I ask. "Did Tarlow tap into the cameras?"

"No cameras in the warehouse are active." Blair sounds a little smug about it, which makes no sense to me. "A few of the soldiers down here didn't come out of the warehouse until after the bombardment finished. They said somebody was ferrying helmets in and telling them to find their way to airlocks leading to the subterranean levels."

Brice elbows me. "Gossip time is over, buddy."

"Gotta go, Blair. The show is starting." I reset my comm. Now I'm only listening on the channel with Brice and my new squad. It's all I'm going to have attention for.

Chapter 22

"The Trogs are here," it's one of our female volunteers, Graham.

"Same on this side," says a guy named Marshall.

"Circle the wagons," Brice tells them all.

My railgun is up, pointed at the stairwell. I expect the Trogs from sub one will be coming out to join the attacking horde, unless they're only down there to block our escape.

One of the troops comes flying through the hangar two meters off the ground, rounding a corner and zipping toward us.

"Slow down," Brice advises.

She manipulates the grav control on her d-pad and clumsily reduces her speed as she collides with a hoist framework.

I hear her grunt over the comm, and it sounds like she's hurt.

"Graham," Brice asks, wearing his battle calm now, "you okay?"

"Bruises. That's it." She's embarrassed.

The other two troops fly toward our position.

"Fliers?" I ask, cutting a glance at Brice. "Is it luck that our volunteers have grav skills good enough to get off the ground?"

He shakes his head as he scans for targets with his weapon. "You ask the right questions, you get the right answers. Then you *volun-tell 'em* what they're going to do." He glances at me to gauge my reaction.

I focus down my barrel. I'm not judging.

"I gave them a chance to back out." He chuckles. "You earned a reputation for what you did on those Trog cruisers. They'd all have stayed if I'd let them."

I guess my reputation doesn't carry with it the mortality rate of the people who've followed me into battle.

I see a haze of blue, coloring the dust in the distance, between two machines.

Brice aims his weapon at the blue glow and fires a burst of red-hot rounds that deflect and ricochet. "They're maxing power to their chest plates."

That shouldn't surprise anyone who's fired more than a few rounds at a Trog.

Brice shoots again and then thumbs behind him. "You, Graham, and Marshall take that half of the warehouse. Wilkes, you're with me."

I spin around and look past a disassembled grav lift, searching for the blue glow that'll mark the presence of the horde.

Graham fires first, working the bolt-action to chamber another round so quickly her hands are a blur. She sends three more rounds downrange in as many seconds. They all deflect.

Marshall fires in another direction, sporadic and slow.

"We just want to delay them," Brice reminds us. "Don't waste too much A and H." He's talking about ammunition and hydrogen in our reactors' fuel cells.

I fire full-auto, not a short burst, and not a sweep across the diffused glow of blue disruptors—at a single point. Rounds skew away from my target in every direction until my deadly red streaks overwhelm a Trog I still can't see. I'm rewarded as my rounds stop flying wildly away and disappear into the mass. The slugs are deflecting into the torsos, arms, and legs as the Trogs' combined field falls into disarray.

As quickly as I can, I trade out an empty magazine and start to fire in short bursts. No more full-auto. We can't kill all of these Trogs, even if we did have an unlimited supply of ammo and H. We need to drag this battle out for as many seconds as we can.

CHAPTER 23

Every dusty gap is glowing a blue that's increasingly brighter, closer.

The ill-defined profiles of Trogs are visible, shaking their weapons, shoving and inching toward us.

"They're going to charge," explains Brice. "Everybody down. It's time to blow the C4."

I duck behind a pile of looped steel tracks that look like they came off a giant earthmoving machine.

"Fire in the hole!" shouts Brice.

I can't help but think, "There's no hole."

The ground shakes.

No sound, of course.

Waves of shrapnel from every direction tear through the hangar above us, each pushing a hazy blast wave of dust particles, gravel, and the expanding gases from the C4's detonation. I feel hundreds of impacts hammer the stack of heavy tracks I'm leaning against.

Trogs' body parts spin through the slurry.

Gales of red gas—vaporized blood—diffuse through the dust, staining it in shades of brown.

"Max grav!" yells Brice. "On me!" He flies off the hangar floor and zips toward the hole in the ceiling we've designated as our escape route.

Wilkes and Graham are instantly in the air, tentatively following Brice's path.

I lift off slowly, looking to make sure Marshall is coming. He's not in the spot where he was concealed as the shooting started. I know he didn't take off with the others. I can't delay. I'm in danger with each second I drift slowly upward. A Trog with his senses not diminished by the blasts could be sighting a railgun on me.

I cast my eyes about, searching.

I spot orange below, drifting. It's Marshall. His body is bent unnaturally, faceplate cracked. His suit is outgassing through a handful of holes, and his body is off the floor, twisting from the jets of escaping air.

His face looks surprised, insulted, uncertain. Not dead.

I stop my ascent.

Do I help?

I diagnose from a distance of four meters.

Marshall's eyes catch mine, pleading for a hand.

If I try to help, at best, I'll prolong his suffering, and I might spend my life for the effort.

Callous and quick, I run the math. It adds up to 'Sorry, brother. You're dead.'

Trogs are starting to move on the ground in every direction. Many wounded. Plenty are shell-shocked. The distraction the C4 charges earned us is evaporating quickly.

I glance toward the hole through the roof. Brice, Wilkes, and Graham are out of sight. I amp up my grav and arc after them as red-hot railgun slugs tear through the suspended dust around me.

I misjudge my speed and bounce into the side of the tunnel through the slag piled on the roof. I pinball into open space over the hangar, spinning and fighting to orient myself upright. My concentration is on Marshall and his wounds, rather than flying.

"Kane," calls Brice. "Over here."

Like that expression means anything over the radio. I look around.

"Other way," Graham shouts.

"What the hell's wrong with you?" demands Brice.

I spot them, through the haze of dust and blast particles. If they'd gone another ten meters farther from the hole, they'd be invisible to me.

"Hurry," Brice orders, his voice turning to concern. "Marshall?"

"Hit." I accelerate toward them.

Wilkes is calling to Marshall over the comm.

In a flash, I'm among the three of them, setting my feet on the roof. "Marshall won't make it." I shake my head. "Not more than a few moments."

Wilkes looks at me, defiant. He glances at Brice. "I'm going back in."

Brice tells him to stay, but Wilkes is already flying toward the hole through the hangar roof and doing it badly.

"Stop!" I yell.

Wilkes ignores us both and veers down into the hangar.

Graham looks at me and then Brice, not knowing how to react.

I don't know either.

Brice grits his teeth and grabs Graham's arm. "Stay here."

"Are you going?" she asks.

"No," he tells her before glancing at me.

"He's fucked up." I'm talking about Marshall, but I don't know if Brice's glance is a question about Marshall's condition or an accusation for leaving him down there. "Lots of holes in his suit. He's probably already dead."

"Wilkes," Brice calls over the comm.

No answer.

"Wilkes."

Railgun rounds shoot out of the tunnel.

"Wilkes!"

Brice shakes his head and turns his attention back to Graham and me.

Just like that, we've put two-thirds of our small volunteer squad into the casualty column.

"Stay close." Brice starts to rise.

I reach out to grab him. "Let's auto grav and stay on the asteroid's surface. We should run."

He stops.

Graham is still looking toward the hole we came through. She hasn't accepted the certainty that Wilkes and Marshall are dead.

"If we get too far out of this shit," I tell them, as I wave a hand at the dust and rocks in the air, "if the Grays in that cruiser see us flying around, they might start shooting again. We have no defense against a bombardment."

"There's no reason they won't fire on us anyway," Brice spits, as his feet come back down on the roof.

I end the discussion by taking off at a sprint.

They both follow.

Chapter 24

We lose our way.

At least it seems we do.

We've been moving a long while. More dumbass déjà vu.

Why did I think running through this gray shit would work out better than walking?

Still, I run.

Floating rocks and pebbles bounce off my faceplate, granular gray in every shape and size. I plow into a stone the size of an end table. Its ragged surface jabs me in the gut, and I double over and tumble with it as I silently curse the advice Brice gave me to reduce my suit's defensive grav.

I disengage from the rock, come to a stop with my ass on the ground, gasping for breath, looking around.

I'm alone.

How the hell did that happen? They were right with me two seconds ago.

The big rock that assaulted me with its inconvenient stagnancy slowly drifts.

Light-g is one thing, but mass and relative velocity still add up to *ouch*. How long has it been since I last cursed Newton and his goddamn Three Laws of Motion?

Damn, he's a fucker.

I adjust my defensive grav for what seems like the tenth time in the last two hours and try to find my bearings. Still not enough air in my lungs.

I realize I don't know which direction is which. My ass is on solid asteroid rock, so I know which way is down.

A sharp pain near my sternum makes me guess I have broken a rib. Or a developing hypochondriac tendency.

Two figures materialize out of the slurry, Brice and Graham.

Brice drops to a knee beside me, weapon at his shoulder, scanning. "Did you see where it came from?"

Graham is down by me, clutching at my arm, and turning my helmet to face hers. "Are you okay?"

I'm still catching my breath, I guess, because I can't push out a whole word yet. I point at the damned aggressive boulder. It's a full meter beyond my reach.

"It was the rock?" she asks, surprised, not quite believing me.

I nod, and draw a deep breath to reset my respiratory system.

"He ran into a rock, Sergeant."

"A rock?" Brice has a hand on my shoulder, checking to see if I'm in one piece. Still looking for Trogs, he spots the stone I collided with, and then he chuckles. "That one?"

I nod.

"We need to slow down," he tells me. "I'll lead. You behind me. Graham, in the rear. Stay close."

I brush away their caregiver hands and stand myself up, thankful for the minimal g.

"Are you sure you're okay?" He's concerned.

It was just a damn rock.

"We can haul you," offers Graham.

I look down at myself. "You see any holes? Air leaking out?"

"No." Graham is shaking her head as she gives me a quick exam. "Broken ribs? Can you breathe okay? You sound like you're having trouble."

"The wind was knocked out of me, is all." I draw another deep breath.

"Let's go," says Brice.

No time to wallow in my bruises. It's my turn to follow.

Brice sets out at a fast walk, scanning from side to side, weapon ready to kill anything that's not a rock.

I'm looking, watching for gravity flux—indications of moving masses—things I know Brice can't see. How I missed that damned floating boulder, though, I can't say. Maybe I invested too much focus ten or twenty yards ahead, hoping to catch sight of Trogs before they spotted me. They have to be hunting us. They have to know we got away.

Phil comes to mind. So does Penny.

The math calculator in my head, the one quantifying a non-numerical world into digits that add up to shitty conclusions, tells me Phil and Penny are dead. It's all about odds and evidence. However, my heart doesn't agree. It says, 'No sweat, don't give up hope.'

It's not hope.

There's something more.

"I think I'm having motion sickness," says Graham.

Brice stops and turns.

Suddenly, we're in a huddle, looking at one another.

Graham is keying her d-pad. "I can't get the medical screen to activate. I'd suck a dick for a dose of Dramamine right now."

I take her hand and pull her arm over to look. I try to navigate to the medical screen. It won't come up.

Fucking shit equipment.

"It's the dust and the rocks," Brice says to Graham. "It's all flowing, throwing off your sense of equilibrium. Don't look around while you walk. Keep close to Kane. Focus on his feet, or his back. You'll be fine."

Graham takes a deep breath. "Seems like we've come a long way."

Brice glances around. "Yeah."

"Probably wandered right past the Trogs," she speculates, "and past the rest of the colony's surface buildings."

"Maybe." Brice looks at me. I was in the lead. I fucked it up. He doesn't say anything about that, but I know he's thinking Graham is right.

I close my eyes, and focus on the gravity.

"Are you okay?" asks Graham.

"Bug-head," Brice informs her.

I tell them, "With all this shit in the air, it's hard for me. I'm straining to see the geography through the gravity of its mass."

"Can't you just see it?" she asks. "Isn't that how it works for you people?"

I feel like I should come up with a clarifying analogy to help her understand. I can't afford to burn the mental bandwidth on that right now. Maybe later. I point to our left. "Over there. Something that way."

"*Something* isn't necessarily a good thing." Brice stares warily into the haze. "How far? What is it?"

"Sixty meters," I tell him. "It could be a hunk of rock, a crashed ship, or a pile of bodies." I glance at them both. "It's something too big to be a Trog, too stationary to be a formation of them out looking for us."

Brice shrugs and walks in the direction I indicated.

I follow with Graham on my heels, wondering if we've walked ourselves out of the battle and right into uselessness.

My thoughts wander back to Phil again. He'd see through this shit. No doubt.

With all the death I've seen since I stepped off that grav lift in Arizona, it seems foolish to believe he's still alive. Death up here in the void is easy. Every misstep is fatal, every wound catastrophic. We're all walking a decision tree of terminal outcomes. Some branches are short. Hell, who am I kidding? It's a goddamn drought-stunted shrub. Only luck's unfair relationship with the bold has kept any of us alive so far.

We've covered maybe half the distance to the mass.

"Can you make it out yet?" asks Brice.

"Definitely not organic," I answer, though I've already assured them no Trogs were ahead.

"That's something." Brice doesn't slow. He trudges forward.

Peering forward with my implant, I make a further deduction. "I think it's not a rock, either."

"One of the buildings?" asks Graham, hopeful.

I nod, though Brice doesn't see, and probably Graham doesn't either. Unfortunately, a lifetime of earthly communication habits don't die easy.

Halfway closer again, and Brice asks, "Do you see any other buildings?"

I stop, close my eyes and look into the distance, trying to piece together shapes out of the mess of grav fields. "Nothing."

Brice looks around, like he might see something with his naked eyes. "This building is out here by itself?"

"Seems that way."

"Let's go see what it is," says Graham, advising us to bypass Brice's growing caution. Her motion sickness is influencing her choice.

Brice looks at me, silently asking my opinion on the matter. I nod toward the building. What other choices do we have?

He's wary, but it's the best option. He turns and leads us on.

Chapter 25

Trudging through the endless dusty crud reveals only that the building has a relatively intense gravity signature. Like most of the roofs on the surface structures, this one is layered deep with two meters of mining slag. The walls are unusual. They're thick, way too thick, if their only purpose is to support the roof in the asteroid's merciful gravity.

The building itself seems to be thirty meters square with a single floor and no tunnel beneath connecting it to the mining operation's sublevels. I have no guesses for what's inside.

I keep all that to myself. We're close enough that speculation time is over. We need to see what this place is.

One corner of the building comes into sight first—a tall, vertical line, out of place in the chaotic flow of asteroid debris. The walls resolve as we step closer. We veer left, following Brice's guess as to which wall has a door.

"Correct," I tell him as I sense the break in the wall where the squat structure's thick metal door stands closed.

A few moments after walking down the front of the building, Brice sees the entrance. He steps away from it, pointing his weapon at the crudely cast obstruction. Graham and I fan out beside him, ready to shoot.

"No airlock," I tell them, in case they haven't guessed already. The door looks more like one of the assault doors on our ships than a precisely sized hatch to an airlock. A triangular graphic, scratched and discolored, marks the door at face level. I can't tell what it is, except maybe a representation of a giant asteroid colliding with a planet as it explodes into space.

It makes no sense.

Brice giggles.

I turn to see an expression of genuine happiness on his face.

"Explosives?" speculates Graham.

"Looks that way to me," agrees Brice.

I guess I'm the only one who didn't pick up on it.

Brice steps back, keeping his rifle aimed at the door. He glances at me, instructing me to do the same. To Graham, he says, "Open it."

We step into position.

As I stand, waiting for what's coming, I find myself contemplating the wisdom of pointing my railgun at a cache of explosives.

The door swings open.

Lights inside flicker on, casting everything in a uniform, daylight glow.

Nothing moves.

Brice is already stepping forward, sweeping his gun's barrel in wider and wider arcs as he passes through the open entrance.

Right behind him, I step in, too.

The interior is neatly arranged with rows of pallets, most piled chest-high with five-gallon buckets, strapped together to keep them secure. Shelves line three walls, containing buckets, boxes, and odd pieces of equipment designed for purposes for which I can only guess.

Brice and I make a quick circuit of the building and find no Trogs. No miners. No grunts.

"Is there an airlock in here?" Brice asks.

I think I already know the answer. Still, I lower my rifle and examine the map of sublevel one.

Graham closes the door behind us. "No sense letting too much of that dust in here."

"Good thinking." I try to place where we are on the surface relative to the subterranean levels. "I'm pretty sure none of the tunnels come anywhere near here."

Brice is walking the interior perimeter, scanning up and down the rows, taking moments to scrutinize individual buckets and drums. "Industrial blasting chemicals," he muses. "There's a shit-ton of it here."

"Maybe a depot for the other colonies?" I guess. And why not, the place seems to have been built as much as a service base for nearby colonies as a mine. Which is probably why the Free Army chose it for their base—infrastructure that could easily be converted to support a small fleet of warships.

Brice finishes his survey of the building and marches back to stand in front of me. "Are you thinking what I'm thinking?"

"Weapons?" I guess. I hadn't been thinking anything, not until he mentioned it.

"Are you okay?" he asks. "You seem kind of out of it."

My shoulders slump at the acknowledgment. I'm tired, as tired as I've ever been.

Brice grabs my left arm and pulls it out while twisting so that my d-pad faces up. He points to a little green button built into one corner of the bezel. "Suit Juice. You used any yet?"

I know what some of the drugs in the cocktail are. I know how addictive they can be. "I don't need—"

Brice pushes the button.

I feel a prick on my thigh where the suit's inner liner houses a series of injectors, with one specifically for this purpose.

Almost immediately, I feel my fatigue melt away, and a burst of confidence radiates through every cell in my body.

I'm a god.

I'm a fucking god of war!

Bow before me lowly creatures in my universe before I smite you and your progeny to Hell!

"Stop grinning." Brice laughs. "You look like an idiot."

I don't stop. I don't care.

"First few times, you get high," he says. "After a while, you just get a few more miles out of the tank."

Too bad. I'm looking across the piles of buckets and barrels on the pallets, and nothing about it is familiar, no sticks of red dynamite, no Play-Doh slabs of C4. In fact, the building looks to be filled with ingredients more than finished products. "Any idea how this stuff works?"

Brice shakes his head. "I know military stuff. Not this shit."

We both look at Graham.

Her eyes go wide. "I worked on a chicken farm before my number came up."

Turning back to Brice. The next step is obvious, at least to me. "Tarlow. He was an explosives guy, right?"

"I think that's what he said."

I comm link to Blair. "Can you hear me? Do we have a signal?"

"I've got you in—" Blair seems lost.

Tarlow picks up for her. "The explosives bunker."

"Is that what this is?" Blair doesn't seem to believe him.

"It is," he confirms. "We keep it far from the colony in case it all blows. That's just administrator paranoia. They don't understand the components or the chemical processes involved. It can't spontaneously detonate. Not in a vacuum. Impossible. You can't tell—"

"Put a plug in it," I order Tarlow. Time to put my divine energy to work for the good of mankind before the drug wears off. "Blair, can you do without Tarlow down there?"

"Why?" She's not pleased, not at all.

"I need him. He's the explosives guy, right?" I scan across the trove of combustibles. "We've got a warehouse of goodies here, and Tarlow can make them useful."

Chapter 26

We're waiting again.

There's a lot of boredom in war.

Blair is sending some of our soldiers from the control center to bring Tarlow to the explosives shed.

Graham is still lying on her back, trying to control her nausea, or napping. She hasn't said anything in a while. It could be either.

Brice is fumbling through what I guess are blasting caps, a variety of types, in a series of translucent bins. He cocks his head toward Graham. "She gonna be alright?"

"I suppose." I'm looking at the bin he has a hand in, realizing I have no guesses about the functions of these odd doodads, no idea how they puzzle together to form something lethal. "You know how this stuff works?"

"In theory."

I laugh. "You mean you'd blow us all up if you tried to rig a bomb?"

"More like I'd build a dud." Brice is one-hundred-percent serious again. "Wouldn't matter. Failure is death out here in the 'stroids. No room to fuck up. If your booby trap doesn't blow, the Trogs swarm you. Death. See what I mean?"

Booby traps sound appealing, however, I'm cultivating my ideal fantasy outcomes into something that'll pass for a plan.

Brice seems suddenly bored, impatient, as he empties his hands. "We should wait on Tarlow."

I agree, look around at the contents of the explosives hut, and start a slow walk along the shelf-covered wall, taking in what I can see, looking for anything I might learn while killing time, and trying not to think about other soldiers out there on the surface, still dying.

"A lot of waiting," says Brice, coming along beside me.

"What do you do to kill the time?" I ask, not wanting to spend too much time with my thoughts, afraid of what I might find in my heart if I dwell on the echoes of last gasps over the comm and vivid memories of dying faces, watching the vacuum suck blood through gaping tears in suits.

"Tell me about Phil," says Brice.

That's a surprising twist.

I hesitate.

I guess at a motive and realize I've spent too much time looking for hidden agendas throughout my life. Too many years in a Gray-ruled world. It's shaped me in a way I didn't realize had bent towards paranoia until just now. "The Phil thing is complicated."

"It always is for people who think too much." Brice smiles after setting the barb. He slaps me on the back to let me know it's just good fun.

I smile, too. No big deal. He's right. I don't want to talk about Phil. "What about you? What's your story?"

"So that's how it works?" he asks. "You won't tell me yours unless I tell you mine?"

"You know a lot more about me than I know about you."

"There's nothing to tell," says Brice. "You already know my dirty laundry. I fragged a captain. You saw me do it."

"So what else have you got?"

"Two years of watching people die in this war." He tries to be hard when he says it, attempting to cover his sadness with a cavalier smile. "Three years of cush garrison duty on the moon after I joined the SDF and before the war started. Four years in construction before that."

"Nine years in space?" It doesn't seem possible anyone could live up here that long.

"I've been wearing an orange suit for a third of my life," he answers.

"Why go that way in the first place? Everybody knows the dangers of wearing orange."

"Same reason you got a bug in your head," he tells me.

"My mom agreed to that before I was a week old," I laugh. "I didn't have a choice."

"Still, your mom had a reason for doing it, right?"

I nod.

"She ever tell you what that was? Or did she think you might grow up to be one of them?"

"That's kind of it," I answer. "The same for both questions. My mom was a laborer, and she wasn't stupid. She knew I wouldn't turn into a Gray if they put a bug in my head, but she saw the writing on the wall. With the Grays in charge of the earth, my mom figured out pretty early that humans were going to become draft horses bridled to the Grays' ambitions. Human life was going to become short and sweaty."

"She was right about that," observes Brice."

"My mom didn't want that for me."

"You grew up and went to work in a grav factory," Brice counters. "Still a slave, right? Roomy house? Plenty to eat?"

I pat my flat belly. "More food than most, I suppose, not as much as you'd think."

"Phil looked like he never missed a meal," argues Brice. "He worked in that grav factory with you, right?"

Looked? Worked?

Both past tense.

Brice rightly thinks Phil is dead.

Could he have survived that collision? Is he out there, adrift? Injured?

Lies I'm telling myself to pretend he's not gone.

"We had privileges." I don't feel ashamed admitting it. The advantaged life of the bug-heads on earth isn't a secret. "We had things to trade on the black market. Phil… I don't know. It's hard to blame Phil for being heavier." I laugh, and I realize it sounds like Brice's dark laugh. Am I picking up the habit from him, or is it something about being in the company of death that makes humor so black?

"How's that?"

"You know, you've seen the old videos, right?"

"From before the siege?" Brice asks. "What's that got to do with anything?"

"People back then, in western countries especially, so many of them were overweight."

"What?" Brice shakes his head. "I don't know what shows you watched but I always imagined before the siege, everybody was perfect. I didn't see many old vids, but in the ones I saw, that's what was there. Perfect hair. Perfect teeth. Perfect clothes. Everybody drove a shiny car."

"Not the movies and TV shows," I clarify. "The news. Documentaries. Stuff that showed real life."

Brice shrugs.

"America used to be the most powerful nation on the planet. Back then the people had everything they ever wanted. Their biggest problems were overeating, drinking too much, and spending all their savings."

Brice appears perplexed.

"You never watched the old news vids?" I can't believe it. "Never had an interest in history?"

"Never had a TV," says Brice. "Wouldn't matter if we did. I worked when I got home from school. I worked from sunup to sundown when they cut me loose after sixth grade."

"No TVs in your school?"

"Some," he answers. "We never saw anything about history. The TVs were for the kids on the high school prep track. Most of us were bound for the farms. You don't need a TV to teach kids how to spell and count, add and subtract. Mostly school was a babysitting service, a place to keep us while our parents worked in the fields, at least until we were big enough to work ourselves. So I don't know what you're talking about. I suppose I've seen some pictures here and there, heard stories about how things used to be, but you know, I never believed half of them, just old-timers pining for the old days. They always make things seem better than they were."

"They were probably telling the truth."

Brice sighs. "I suppose. All that perfect hair and those perfect teeth must have meant something. What's that got to do with Phil?"

"I guess I don't want you to think Phil's problems are all his."

"Whatever you say."

I lean on a pallet of explosives, maybe enough to blow all of Breckenridge into orbit. I comm link to Blair. "Is Tarlow coming?"

"Not yet," she tells me. "We're trying to coordinate down here."

"People are dying," I remind her. Even I feel like an asshole for saying it.

Her response is testy. "I'm not sending my people headlong into an ambush. We'll do this right or not at all."

"Yes, Colonel."

Blair huffs. "We have another two dozen or so down here. More on the way. Not nearly as many died in the bombardment as we thought."

"Are they armed?"

"Mostly," she tells me, "with disruptors and single-shot railguns."

"Okay." I figure it's best not to push any harder. "Let me know when Tarlow leaves."

Brice is looking at me with an odd expression on his face.

"What?"

"I'm riveted by this story of Phil's weight problem." He sounds vaguely sarcastic, but I'm not sure. "It might be the most interesting story I'll hear all day."

I'm not sure I want to say anything more about it. I sit on a pallet of large metal buckets. They all sport labels covered with warnings and directions, fine print—thousands of words no one will ever read. Looking around inside the bunker for any distraction, I realize for the tenth time, there isn't much to do while waiting. So, I talk. "He had a brother."

"Lots of people do."

"They were both bug-heads," I tell Brice.

"How long have you known him?"

"We were in school together, all of the "special" kids. Pre-school, I guess. They started us young. I've always known Phil."

"What's this brother got to do with anything?" Brice wickedly smiles. "Did Phil eat him?"

I shake my head. "He died when he was six."

Brice feels bad about his off-color joke, but I don't make a thing of it. We don't have vaccinations like they did before the siege. We don't have antibiotics, not in a large enough supply for everyone. We don't have much in the way of medicines, not for anybody who's not Korean. Lots of babies die. Lots of kids don't make it adulthood. Death is always around. You get used to it.

CHAPTER 27

"They told us the news over at the hospital." I start, thinking of the smells in that place, like a closed-up house with no breeze where rats have been trapped with mounds of their shit and only an acrid hint of antiseptic to make it seem like the air is safe to breathe. I can taste it. I remember how the funk clung to my clothes and followed me through the rest of the day. "The doctors told his parents it was an immune reaction to the bug in his head. Like with me and Phil, they put the bug in his brother's head when he was a baby, but it never took. His body never accepted it. Then, when his lymphocytes couldn't kill it—got tired of trying I guess—they went insane and turned on him."

Brice grimaces.

"The doctors had big words for it all. I'm not going to claim I understood everything." I don't know why the disclaimers are important, they just seem like they are. "Phil's brother was sick all the time, as his body was eating itself up from the inside. It took years for him to die, while his organs struggled to develop into a regular person. It just failed. He grew up disproportionally. He was always small and skinny compared to other kids his age, but his head kept growing. Just the bones, not the skin. It looked like one day his face might stretch so tight it would split open when he laughed or coughed." I take a breath, even though I'm feeling the amphetamine cocktail still coursing through my blood, the story is bringing me back to that time, unreeling like a poorly edited movie in my head, full of abstract emotions.

"I went with them to the doctor many times. I don't know why. I was a kid. I went along because an adult brought me. It never seemed weird until the thought came back to me as a grownup." I glance up at Brice and see he's paying attention because this next part is important, at least to me. "I know Phil's mom wanted to believe the doctors were trying to help his little brother but they weren't. They were taking measurements and running tests. They wanted to understand everything about their little patient, to know what was making him tick. To them, he was nothing more than an experiment, and they weren't going to give him any drug that might harm the bug or kill it."

"How do you know that?" asks Brice. "Did they tell you?"

The question takes me off guard, because I realize I don't know the answer. I never heard a doctor say those things. No one in Phil's family ever offered up any evidence for their suspicions, yet Phil believed it strongly, and so did his dad. The old man went on about it with tinfoil hat tenacity, at least when Phil's little brother and mother weren't around. I answer Brice with something vague. "Things I heard."

Brice accepts my answer and nods to prompt me on.

"The kid died. It was the flu that finally finished him off one winter. I remember Phil crying a lot. His mom tumbled into a black mood she never recovered from. His dad took to working more, or finding ways to avoid coming home. I almost never saw the old man after that."

"I've been to funerals for kids," says Brice. "They're never easy."

"There wasn't a funeral." Even as a kid, that seemed unusual to me. "The doctors bagged up Phil's brother and took him away, telling Phil's parents he was the property of the MSS. Just like that. No grave. No service. Nothing."

"Damn shame," says Brice.

He's right.

"An unusual thing happened after that," I say. "The food ration for Phil's brother never stopped coming. I know I'm exaggerating when I say it, but to me, it seemed like Phil's mother made Phil eat every bite of it. After watching one child waste away, a skinny kid was the most horrid thing she could imagine. She blamed herself, ultimately she had to, I guess. She chose to let the Grays put the bug in her kids' heads. She turned into love-overkill mom, stuffing Phil with every crumb she could find, protecting him from skinned knees, other kids' meanness, bug bites, you name it. If she could have wrapped him in a papoose and carried him around on her back, I think she would have."

"And he got bigger?" asks Brice, trying to be unusually polite.

"Chubbier with each passing year. At school, kids teased him." I look at Brice, because I know he knows this. "You never see fat kids anywhere, anymore. You rarely see obese adults. Not enough food left on earth after we ship everything to the moon colony or orbital battle stations, or the mines in the asteroid belt, or the SDF, or the construction crews, or fucking North Korea. Not enough people left on earth to grow what's needed." I shrug. "People, not just kids, resented Phil for his weight. It changed him. Made him—"

"Prickly?" Brice suggests.

"Yeah." It's a fitting word.

At a stopping point in Phil's history, we don't say anything for a while.

I call Blair again for an update on Tarlow's progress, and she promises me he's on the way.

Still, nothing more to say.

We stare and wait, until another of my memories comes up that I haven't thought about for a long time. "You know, I saw one die once."

Chapter 28

"You saw a Gray die?" Brice is skeptical. It's something every human dreams about seeing, however, the layers of elegant sincerity wrapped around most stories of dead Grays fall away under questioning, exposing the wistful rumor beneath.

My story is real, though, not something I heard about, something I saw.

The incident is clear in my mind like it just happened. "I was thirteen then. I lived down near Silverthorne before the spaceport grew up to take over the whole valley. In those days, every mine with a kilo or two of ore still in the ground was being worked to support the grav factories and shipyards. Trailers to house the miners were spread over every flat meadow and muddy riverbank through the mountains.

"My mom and me lived in a row of identical trailers, two-room boxes on wheels packed tightly on three acres of bare dirt a few blocks uphill from the Blue River. She slept in the bedroom. I used the couch in the other room, which doubled as our living room and kitchen. Phil lived two houses down with his parents and brother, four of them in a place identical to ours.

I half chuckle. "It seems shitty now to live in such cramped squalor." I look at Brice. He knows the privileges bug-heads get, so I don't feel like I'm bragging. I don't know what I feel about it. "Now I have a house with an upstairs and a basement with a grassy lawn and trees. Three people on three floors, each twice the size of those trailers we lived in."

"Your mom made the right choice putting a bug in your head," says Brice. "The house I grew up in sounds a bit like your trailer, but no wheels. It was rotting right out from underneath us. My dad was always scrounging wood and scrap sheet metal to fix holes in the roof and floor."

For a moment, it seems Brice is nostalgic for it. Maybe I am, too. Squalor isn't bad when it's all you know. At least life had a simplicity to it then, the only worry was constant hunger. Even the MSS seemed like a problem for parents to deal with, not kids.

"I didn't realize it until I was in fourth or fifth grade—everybody who lived on the three-acre dirt plot had bug-headed kids—the MSS had long since relocated the miners who lived there before us. The Grays wanted us kids to play together, to form pods or whatever. We were an experiment, members of the first generation of implanted humans with a bug since birth. There were a dozen colonies of us around the valley, yet all of us kids attended the same school. We didn't have any normal friends. They kept those kids separate from us, at least until they moved them all out of the Gray Zone."

"A Gray Zone?" Brice asks. "I haven't heard that phrase since I was a kid. What is a Gray Zone?"

"That's what they called it in those days, Breckenridge and places like it," I answer. "It was supposed to be an area safe for the Grays." I laugh at the bleak reality of earth's situation. "Now the whole planet is a Gray Zone. It didn't take long for that to happen—a single generation."

"Safe for Grays." Brice is just as disgusted by the state of the world. "Not so much for people."

"It was summer," I continue, getting back on track with my story. "Me and Phil were riding our bikes up to Frisco. We were headed toward town to meet up with a couple kids we knew from school, and the three of us wanted to hike up the mountain and follow the ridges south down Tenmile Range, hitting all the peaks along the way until we reached Hoosier Pass. We were stupid enough to think we could do the whole hike by midday and make it back home in time for dinner." I laugh, genuinely. "Probably a good thing we never got up the mountain that day."

"How's that?" asks Brice.

"No way we could made it back. We'd have ended up missing days of school. The MSS would have punished our parents."

Brice grimaces. Everybody knows about the MSS's brutal discipline.

"It was still early." I remember the way the sun felt hot on my face even though the air was still cool. It had been a dry summer. There wasn't any moisture in the air to take the edge off the sun's harsh glare. "Me and Phil had just rolled down the dirt road, not pedaling more than a few times on the downhill zigzag to the bridge across the river.

"The spaceport wasn't as busy then as it is today. Earth's industry was only a dozen years past the siege and was still ramping up to meet the Grays' needs. Still, big semis hauled shipments along Highway 9 in what seemed like an unending slow line on the rough road. All that cargo was destined for the grav lifts to be shot into orbit for construction of the space station.

"We stopped at the corner of the two-lane highway, in the parking lot of the ration distribution center. The trucks were loud and slow, with one rolling by every thirty or forty seconds. Dust was in the air so thick it got in your eyes, and you could taste the grit in your mouth. Half the asphalt on the road had crumbled away because the Grays had no interest in fixing it. We were waiting for a gap between the trucks so we could cross. Mostly, we were just watching the semis, because the truth was, there was enough space between them we could have crossed any time. Phil saw it first, and pointed it out to me. He always had a good sense for when Grays were around."

"He saw the dead Gray?" Brice asks.

"No," I answer. "Not dead yet."

Chapter 29

"To me," I tell Brice, "Grays seem fragile when they walk, like really old women, feeble and slow, like they might fall over and die at any moment. Except Grays don't fall over, they just keep on moving, like ants that don't give up. Have you ever seen one run?"

Brice nods.

I go on to describe it. "Grays don't run like anything on earth, not any animal or even any bug that I've seen. They stiffen like boards and they kind of bounce from foot to foot with their legs spread wide. They remind me of a kid I saw in an old movie with braces on his legs. So, when Phil pointed out the pod of Grays and said one of them was acting strange, I turned to look, but I figured I'd see a Gray acting like they always do."

"But that's not what you saw," guesses Brice.

Shaking my head, I tell him, "One of them was walking in circles and swatting at the air. Its head rolled around on its thin neck. I thought at first its neck was broken. Then it would stiffen for no reason at all and run. Directionless. Phil was starting to freak out about it, which I thought was weird, like he felt sorry for it." I shake my head again. "I didn't know at the time how strongly he could connect to them, or to any of us for that matter."

That's when I realize why I keep entertaining the notion that Phil isn't dead. He doesn't feel absent like his brother did the day he died.

I wonder again if I'm telling myself lies.

"It was disturbing," I tell Brice. "In that moment, I felt sorry for it. The other Grays were pogoing on their spindly legs and trying to corral the crazy one to catch it—I'm not sure—to help it, I guess?

"I learned later, they evolved from plants. They don't eat the way we do. They absorb various wavelengths of electromagnetic energy from their surroundings. They suck nutrients through their skin when they touch things. They never had an evolutionary imperative to catch their dinner. Seeing them trying to catch the sick one was like watching blind people trying to capture fireflies."

"Doomed to fail," adds Brice.

"After watching for a few minutes, Phil told me the sick one had Crazy Stick."

"I've seen some contraband vids," says Brice. "That's what it sounds like to me."

I silently confirm and go on to say, "Some bacteria infects their system. Nobody knows if the bacteria is terrestrial in origin or if the Grays brought it with them. It might not be bacteria at all, just that really ancient Grays act like that right before they die."

"I've never heard of anybody doing an autopsy on one." Brice is disappointed over what seems like a wish he'd enjoy fulfilling. "I've only heard rumors about what's inside those little bastards."

I figure Brice is going to like this next part. "Phil and I were still right there in the parking lot when the crazy one made for the road. He ran most of the way across. He wasn't fifteen feet in front of us when one of those big semis locked its rear wheels. The trailer skidded toward where we were standing, not very far, but close enough to scare us. The truck's front bumper knocked the Gray down, and it fell badly, right in front of the front tire.

"It seemed like slow motion, and in a way it was, with the truck finally stopping. The tire caught the Gray's feet and rolled up its legs. The thing's arms went crazy, beating the road and flapping. Phil cried out like he felt every bit of it. I didn't, but I felt something."

"Empathy?" asks Brice.

I shake my head. "Something more elemental than that. Almost like the truck was crushing my legs." I shiver as I recall the sensation. "The tire just kept rolling. I guess the truck had too much momentum to come to a stop. The Gray's head was bouncing up and down on the road like it was trying to beat its own brains out to stop the agony. The tire rolled over the Gray's torso, getting close to the neck, then the top of the Gray's head burst open, exploding orangish-yellow jelly onto the road. It was disgusting. It smelled like an outhouse.

"While the Gray's arms were still twitching, Phil elbowed me and pointed at the other five. They'd all fallen over as if they were dying, too."

Brice is incredulous. "They all died?"

Shaking my head, I answer, "When the squashed Gray stopped convulsing, they started to recover."

"So flattening it with the truck tire," says Brice, "and popping its head like a zit didn't kill it?"

"That orange jelly inside its head is a separate organism living in a symbiotic relationship with the Gray's body. The body died, but the jelly thing lying there on the road in the sun didn't, at least not for a while.

"That made me think about the symbiont in *my* head. It made me wonder what's going to happen to me when it dies."

"How long will the bug in your head live?" asks Brice.

"Nobody has an answer for that question. At least not one they're willing to share with any of us bug-heads." I sigh. "I suppose Phil and me should have run out of there after what we saw, yet we didn't. After a while, the Grays gathered themselves and walked over to stare at their dead buddy. They stayed at a distance. As if they were all afraid of catching Crazy Stick. I don't know.

"Before I realized what was happening, more Grays were there, and the MSS was with them, strutting around in their uniforms with guns on their hips. One was shouting in my face, demanding to know what had happened.

"Phil started answering his questions.

"I kept staring at the dead Gray and its orange marmalade brains on the road, knowing although the Gray was dead, the jelly symbiont wasn't. I felt it there, suffering, rolling in the dust.

"Another Gray, an important one, was suddenly on the scene. It was clear he was important because he had a human interpreter with him, a kid not much older than me and Phil. The kid had been raised with the important Gray since both were babies. The interpreter was able to speak the Gray's thoughts in words we humans were capable of hearing. It was the only way we were truly able to communicate with them.

"The interpreter, 'the mouthpiece', we called him, ordered the MSS officers to take the driver out of the truck.

"The driver hadn't moved from the driver's seat. He was too afraid to come out and see what he'd done even though it wasn't his fault. It was clear to anybody who'd witnessed what had happened, but that didn't matter. A Gray was dead. A human was involved. Case closed.

"The man begged and pointed to Phil and me, saying he could have swerved off the road—to the left, he'd have run over more Grays, to the right, he'd have run over us, waiting on our bikes for our chance to cross.

"The MSS officer glared at us, but ordered his men to drag the driver in front of the truck and hold him down on the ground. Another MSS man climbed into the truck and started it up. They rolled the front tire over the driver. They did it slow. He screamed while the tire flattened his legs. Blood gushed out his mouth when the tire rolled up over his stomach and smashed his chest."

Brice shakes his head. It's an appalling end to the story, but not unexpected.

"We didn't hike that day," I tell him. "Phil and me rode our bikes home, not saying anything along the way.

"Up until then, the occupation had been an abstract thing for us. We lived in the Gray Zone, neither of us had ever seen the destruction out in the rest of the world. We never personally knew anyone who'd died, besides Phil's brother. Our parents worked at low-level jobs at the spaceport or the mines. We usually had food to eat.

"We didn't know injustice and brutality.

"Phil remembered the brutality the most, and he changed after that. It was like something inside him chose to hide itself away and never come out again. We seldom rode much after that, and we never hiked the high mountains. He was afraid of what might be lurking in the woods. He was afraid of the steep drops. He was afraid when the storms came, and he looked at the mountains like the snow might avalanche down at any minute and kill everyone he'd ever met.

"The brutality gave me nightmares that haunted me for years, but where Phil grew scared, I turned reckless, ready to take any dare, because I knew as long as Grays ruled my life, it was worth nothing. And I hated that idea."

The door opens and in walks three orange-clad rebels with Tarlow in tow.

"'Bout time," says Brice.

Chapter 30

Standing by a pallet of stacked buckets, laying his hands on them like they're his special pets, Tarlow says, "This is TX. It's a ternary compound of inert liquids that doesn't turn volatile until mixed."

"Ternary?" Graham asks. "What does that mean?"

"It's got three parts," I answer. "Tarlow's trying to sound smart."

"How volatile?" asks Brice.

"Not like nitroglycerine," answers Tarlow, "but you want to be careful with it."

"That doesn't tell me anything," Brice persists. "Can you drop it? Bump it?"

"Drop it?" Tarlow laughs as he shoves a bucket off the top of the pile. It moves slug-slow toward the floor.

"If you kick it?" I urge. "You know what he's asking. How much abuse can it take?"

"Once mixed," says Tarlow, "any good-sized electrical charge and it will detonate. A static charge might do the trick. So be careful about that, especially with all this dust in the air. You can collect a charge just walking through it, like crossing a carpet in an arid environment back on earth."

"What about concussions?" I ask. "More specific, please."

"You can kick a bucket of it, and nothing happens." Tarlow looks down his nose at each of us. "But put a hot railgun round through it, or land a grav lift on it and you better hope you're nowhere near."

"Okay," says Brice. "That's all sweet and special. How quickly can you mix some of this stuff up and code the detonators to our d-pads?"

Tarlow points to three pallets of buckets that appear to be disorganized. "Those are already mixed." He smiles guiltily. "I'm not supposed to blend this stuff except on demand—it takes a while. In this gravity, you can't pour the buckets out, you have to pump them and," he points at a washing machine-sized piece of equipment that looks like it belongs in a bakery back on earth, "mix them in that before pumping the final product back into the containers."

"Does it separate?" asks Brice.

"Good question." Tarlow grins. "In earth gravity, yes. Four to five days on the shelf is all it takes to make it nearly ineffective. Two weeks after mixing and it won't even burn. Up here, I could let it sit for months before enough separation occurs for the difference to be measurable."

"And you said you blended this when?" I ask.

"Right before the Trogs arrived."

"We're good, then?" confirms Brice.

"Should be," answers Tarlow.

"What do you use all this for?" asks Graham.

Tarlow points up through the roof. "You saw those big asteroids out there? They're all too massive for our tug to push to light speed. We have to make them smaller. We've drilled most of them. What we do is set the explosives in the holes and detonate them simultaneously to split them into transportable chunks."

Which leads to my next question. "How much of this stuff do you think it would take to split that Trog cruiser down the seams?"

CHAPTER 31

The buckets are satisfactory for my purpose, maybe perfect, a metaphor for the measure of my intent and malice.

Either way, the buckets of TX are what Brice and I have to work with—twenty in all, strapped together in two bundles of ten, three hundred and fifty pounds each, a load that would be impossible for us to manually transport back on earth. However, on the Potato, weight is no problem. The momentum is, and needs to be managed.

Three hundred and fifty pounds represents enough mass to crush a human body if it's moving at a decent clip. A little faster, and it might spontaneously detonate on impact. The asteroid is covered with plenty of stone outcroppings, opportunities for such a collision to occur.

After forty-five minutes of carefully handling our loads through the irritating slurry of dust and rock, Brice and I are resting beside a chubby stone mesa near the wide end of the Potato.

"The haze isn't too thick down here," pants Brice.

I'm looking at the sky, able to make out the nearby asteroids, able to see the stern of the Trog vessel still laying claim to its spot of empty space above us.

In five separate liter-sized containers, blasting bottles Tarlow called them, we have TX set to detonate. The bottles are sized to fit down holes drilled deep into asteroids. Each will produce a powerful charge. Brice and I have jammed bottles into the crevices between the pipes and hoses on a drilling rig formerly used for creating holes for the bottles. The rig is standing on the Potato's surface, sixty meters on the other side of the rocky wart keeping Brice and I hidden.

Brice has the detonators on the blasting bottles connected to his d-pad, and he's looking at me now, silently asking if I'm ready.

I notice the elapsed time. "You think the others have had time to get their TX charges down to the sublevels?"

Trying to address my hesitation, he says, "With all the shit in the air fouling the radio links, we knew we'd lose comms when we made it this far out." Still, he waits for an answer. "Does it matter?"

In truth? No.

We have no way of knowing whether the explosion we're about to detonate will trigger a reaction from the Trogs. We don't know the state of the rest of our forces. We've chosen a self-assigned mission that needs to be carried to success if any of us wants to leave this rock alive and free. The only thing I know for a fact.

My eyes settle on Brice, yet my thoughts are focused inward as I reach my decision. "Fuck it."

Brice's smile belies a pyromaniac tendency as he taps the button on his d-pad. A timer starts to tick down through ten seconds. He pats his bundle of buckets. "All we have to hope now is the concussion from the explosion doesn't set this shit off."

Both our bundles are off the ground by a meter or so, not touching anything. They're shielded from blast shrapnel by the rock we're hiding behind. Still, my earthbound intuition of explosions makes me fret.

"Five seconds."

I grav myself into position beneath my bundle and flip around to put my feet on the ground, knees bent, ready to push.

Brice slips beneath his load, just as the timer expires.

The rock beneath us shakes sharply.

Jagged hunks of metal and fragments of stone rip through the dust on both sides of us.

Time to fly.

I push off and assist the strength in my legs with a forceful nudge from my suit's grav plates.

Brice grunts under the strain of pushing the stationary momentum of his load into motion.

We're both off the surface.

In seconds we're above the thickest of the gray slurry, hunks of pollen nestled in the core of the expanding bloom of twisted metal from the explosion we just detonated, hoping the Trogs believe we're part of the debris.

I adjust my grav to aim at the asteroid I think will put us in the best position for our plan, and push my load on the same trajectory. I kill my grav, and relax with legs askew and my arms out to the sides, going ballistic, one more hunk of crap in the solar sphere at the mercy of the gravitational pull of the masses around me.

"You all right?" Brice asks.

"Thanks," I chuckle.

"What?" He has no clue why I'm amused.

"You complimented me," I tell him. "I'm trying to look dead."

"Maybe you should have pursued acting instead of volunteering for this shit."

"They don't have actors anymore."

"In the propaganda films they do," he argues.

"Yeah," I laugh, "*if* I wanted to spend my life pretending to be a dumbass in the films where North Koreans are always doing the smart thing. Not for me."

I realize I'm slowly rotating as the explosion's debris cloud thins. However, I'm past the point where I can risk a grav adjustment or movement. Out here with nothing to shield me from the penetrating eyes of little Gray fucks on that Trog cruiser, I need to maintain the charade. If I don't sell my dead routine, they'll no doubt send a volley of railgun rounds to ensure my demise.

Of course, they might do that anyway.

I lose sight of Brice as I spin, instead satisfying myself with a view of the sparkly diamond of our sun blazing far away at the center of the solar system. It makes me feel so, so far removed from everything. Even the word, 'everything', takes on a different proportion out here with a billion miles of hostile vacuum stretched between me and my home.

Inexplicably, I think of Claire, that smile the first time I saw her, the softness of her skin, the taste of her mouth on mine. The loss of her false love still clenches a brawny fist around my heart and glasses tears over my eyes. No matter how much our marriage was an expedient lie for her, to me, it was the most real thing I ever lived. The death of it still aches. The loneliness from three years of watching her give her entire being to that reeking stick-thing living in my bedroom puts a sharp point on my isolation.

The debris around me starts to thin. My gravitational sensitivities, no longer muffled by the cloud of debris cloying the Potato, feel clear. I no longer need my eyes to picture the three dimensions of space surrounding me.

Brice is there behind me, stiff and playing his own corpse role. Out here with so little mass to skew my senses, I feel his heart beating and see his chest expand with each breath. I can even detect his muscle movements, and see the flow of blood through his veins.

It makes me wonder—how much more clearly than me a Gray can perceive the world? The potential frightens me with its implications.

Pointed in the other direction, the Trog cruiser dominates the sky behind me. Far past, I feel massive Jupiter, slowly spinning inside the halo of its moons.

"That ship is massive," utters Brice.

"Standard size, though, right?" Of course it is.

"That's not what I'm saying," he counters.

"You think we might not have enough to blow it open?" I ask, as I come to accept Brice's worry.

"You know that's what I'm thinking."

"Tarlow said—"

"That's what worries me." Brice makes an exasperated sound. "I know he said we've got plenty to blow the hull open, but you know as well as I do, he's guessing. All his knowledge about the structure and materials in these ships would fit into a Gray's asshole."

Everybody knows Grays don't have sphincters, so I guess that makes Brice's point.

I don't agree, so I wonder whether my acceptance of Tarlow's certainty was a case of me hearing what I wanted to hear.

"I don't like trusting him," says Brice. "He's not dependable."

"He's just different." I slip into Dr. Psychologist mode. "You're projecting other unpalatable traits on him because of one or two characteristics you don't like."

Brice chuckles through a series of joyless noises. "So long as you don't mind me fragging him when this goes to shit. I don't care what you think the reasons are."

That's funny, although not in the way Brice thinks. "If this fails, the Trogs will blow every one of these asteroids to rubble, and we won't have to worry about who's alive when it's over."

We float for a bit in silence, Brice watching the Trog ship, me lazily spinning with a fantastic view of the whole universe.

Brice makes a few attempts to contact Blair by radio, with no response. Neither of us is surprised. That statically charged dust is doing its work.

"'Bout halfway," he informs me.

Our destination asteroid is coming into my view. We're on course to impact it near where we'd planned—on the far side, out of the cruiser's view, and hopefully with enough of the asteroid's mass between us and the ship that the Grays up there won't detect the grav Brice and I use to maneuver our explosives to a soft landing.

"Major?" It's a woman's voice, not Blair.

Startled, I ask, "Who's this?"

"Silva, sir."

"Silva?" I grin through a sense of relief I hadn't expected to feel.

"Where?" asks Brice.

"You're headed toward us," she answers.

"Us?" I ask.

"Lenox and Mostyn are here with me."

"You made it?" It's a stupid thing to say, but sometimes stupid is the best I can come up with when I'm surprised.

"We went for cover when the shooting started."

"Injuries?" I ask.

"None," she tells me. "We're holed up in a mining shack over here near a piece of drilling equipment."

"I see it," says Brice.

The asteroid is slipping out of my line of sight as I spin, but through my grav sense, I can make it out.

"How are you set for A and H?" Brice asks.

"Ammo's fine," answers Silva. "We're topped off on hydro. There's a stock of H packs and C packs in the shed."

"We'll come to you," Brice tells them.

CHAPTER 32

I baby my load down to the surface. With the bulk of the Trog cruiser, an array of defensive grav fields surrounding it, and a few million tons of asteroid rock between us, I doubt the Grays in the bow will detect the grav I'm using to maneuver my suit.

My main concern is after using the mass of an asteroid as cover to sneak up on the Trogs twice, will the Grays be focusing their super sharp grav sense at every nearby asteroid to see what's hiding behind it?

Brice nurses his bundle of TX buckets down to the surface beside me.

Lenox, Mostyn, and Silva are out of the mining shack and coming toward us.

"It's good to see you guys," says Lenox.

I smile, but I find myself staring at Silva, trying to see the shape of a woman inside her bulky orange gear.

She catches me looking at her, and I turn away, busying my hands at uselessly checking the tension on the straps around the buckets.

"We made it this far." Brice punches me in the arm. "Right?"

I look up, and he's smiling. Apparently, he didn't expect this much success. "Yeah," I answer, confidently.

"Hey, boss." Silva punches me in the other arm, and I turn to see she's smiling too, eyes trying to catch mine in a lingering gaze.

Just a moment past the end of my melancholy drift across the void, and I find it's easy to look at her and entertain a thought about what a future might look like with another woman in it. "It's good to see you."

She wraps me in a hug. Lenox and Mostyn embrace us both as much as that can be done in the gear we're all cocooned in.

"I thought we were alone," Lenox admits as she pulls away from me.

"That's okay," offers Brice, as he leans over. "We thought the three of you were blasted off into space."

"We were," Lenox tells him, "but not so far we couldn't recover."

"What about the Rusty Turd?" asks Silva. She's talking about our assault ship. "I can't raise them on the comm."

I shrug and shake my head.

"Destroyed?" asks Lenox.

"Don't know," Brice tells her, glancing at me because he believes there's no open question on the matter.

Lenox follows Brice's look in my direction and guesses wrong on its intent. "Are we stuck here, sir?"

"No." I shake my head to emphasize my certainty on that point. "There are a lot of damaged ships over there on the surface of the Potato, and there are repair shops and parts. And people. We found the station's crew, a few hundred of them in holding pens down on sublevel nine. Once we take care of our Trog infestation, we can probably repair as many of those ships as we want."

Mostyn sighs. She wasn't expecting anything so rosy. Likely, the three of them had concluded they'd be stuck on the small asteroid until they found a way to sneak back to the Potato and hijack something capable of making light speed.

Silva glances at the two erstwhile castaways with her, and then her eyes settle on me. She's investing her hopes. She wants to believe in a happy outcome to all this shit. "What do we need to do?"

Brice points at his feet, down through the asteroid's core, and out the other side, right up through the Trog cruiser's curved aft drive array. "We need to knock that scag out of the sky and neutralize all the Trogs on the surface." He catches himself as he's finishing up. "And the ones underground."

"Do we know how many yet?" asks Lenox, not an ounce of apprehension in her. She's ready, and no doubt understands the risks.

"No. Not a clue." I pat a TX bucket in my bundle. "We have our part of the mission. We'll do it, and then we'll worry about the Trogs on the surface. Once step at a time."

"One step at a time," confirms Brice.

"What's this, then?" asks Silva, squatting down to examine the label on one of the buckets. "Doesn't look promising."

"Industrial explosives," I answer. "They drop it into the bore holes they drill in these asteroids to split them in half." I throw in the last part to emphasize the power of the syrupy-thick liquid in the buckets.

"Powerful," figures Lenox, glancing past us, taking measure of the rock we're standing on.

"They'll do the job." I share a look of what I hope is certainty with Mostyn, and then Silva. I pause when I see doubt in Silva's eyes, probably because she sees the truth of the doubt in mine. "I don't know how strong this stuff is." I acknowledge Brice with a quick look, letting him know I've come around to his way of thinking. "The tech who set all this up for us is in the business of breaking rocks, not star cruisers." I finish with a shrug. Not a great leadership moment, but I'm going to ask these three women to come along on a mission that'll only reduce their already dismal odds of long-term survival.

"Doesn't matter." Brice is certain. "We're going up there, down there, whatever. We'll split that cruiser open and kill all the Trogs in it. If it doesn't work, we'll try the next thing, and the next, and the next."

That's the kind of certainty I can get behind—the certainty of persistence. "We have seven hundred pounds of this stuff." I pat one of the buckets again. "We put it in the right place on that ship, and we'll take it out of action."

Lenox steps up close, and starts to read the label on one of the buckets. "It's a ternary explosive."

I nod.

"Did you mix it?" she asks.

"Do you know about explosives?" asks Brice.

"Only what I've read." She looks at each of us as she straightens back up. "And I know a little bit about bubble jump arrays."

I'm curious. "Go on."

Lenox smiles devilishly. "Knock some of those plates out of alignment and either the ship won't create a well-formed wave and won't be able to bubble jump, or maybe it'll end up on a skewed course and stuck in the interstellar void."

"What are you thinking?" I ask. "Plant these in the drive array?"

"No," she answers. "One, maybe two. Just enough to damage the array in case your plan to destroy the ship doesn't work out. If we can't kill 'em, then fuck them up the ass with a pinecone for coming to our neighborhood and acting like assholes."

I smile my enthusiasm. Nothing wrong with a good backup plan.

CHAPTER 33

Since keeping our feet on the surface of the asteroid is achieved primarily through suit grav to enhance the effect of the local g, I realize walking around to the other side of our small asteroid isn't any stealthier than amping up the g and blazing through the sky. Either way, an attentive Gray worried about the cruiser's rear flank will spot us.

So, we're off the ground again, curving over the horizon as we separate from our big rock. We're all in a line, heading straight toward the Trog cruiser's stern drive array.

I'm in the lead, eyes wide open, grav senses stretched to their limit, trying to see any change as soon as it occurs, believing fluctuations in the cruiser's defensive fields are my proxy warning system for impending danger. Right behind me, Silva is flying with nothing but a weapon in her hands. Mostyn is a few meters back, guiding my bundle of TX buckets. Brice follows her with his bundle. Lenox has the rear with one bucket in hand.

"Stay close," I tell them. "There's a surge in the field coming up. Follow my path exactly, or it'll bounce you out." Deflect them actually, just like a railgun round bending its path away from a Trog's chest plate.

I see a series of donut-shaped fields stacked off the stern of the ship, and I can't help but wonder at the grav talent of some of these Grays for the complexity of the field shapes they're able to coax out of their defensive hull arrays.

I bear left to slip through a gap where two of the donut-shaped fields are neutralized because the polarities flip directions.

Silva grunts like she's been slugged, and I know she's drifted off my course.

"Exact," I remind them. It comes out more angry than urgent. A mistake I don't have time to apologize for. "There's not a lot of room." I slip into a neutral zone in the hole of a donut, come to a stop, and spin around to watch the others follow my path.

Silva floats to a stop beside me with a nod and a smile. Harsh words forgiven. Effortlessly so. Draftees resent officers as part of the natural order of the universe. I decide my easy absolution is due to another reason, one skewed strongly by what I want it to be. I decide she likes me as much as I think I like her.

Christ, do men ever mature past the sweet temptation of pubescent puppy love?

What would be the fun in that?

I need to focus on the mayhem ahead.

Mostyn is slowing and delicately maneuvering her load.

"Another meter forward," I direct her. "Then cut hard toward us."

She listens and moves as told.

Her buckets are buffeted on one side. She squeezes through the gap between the grav fields, and her bundle starts to spin.

Silva accelerates over to help Mostyn bring the load back under control.

Brice squeezes perfectly through the gap—surprising, considering he's unable to see the static grav fields. They're invisible to the normal human, but glow like neon signs to a bug-head like me.

Lenox, with only the single bucket in tow, has little trouble following Brice through.

We're a hundred meters astern of the Trog cruiser, in the neutral hole at the center of a toroidal grav field, the first of a dozen donut-shaped fields stacked smallest to largest from where we are, up to the stern of the vessel.

I point through the series of donut holes toward the cruiser's dormant drive array. In everything but size, it looks like the array on the aft end of the Rusty Turd. Either could be mistaken for the dish of a radio telescope back on earth. "We head right up the axis of the ship now. There's no grav to repel us unless we drift off the centerline. Once we arrive at the ship, we slip over the lip of the array, move onto the outer hull and grav compensate. The whole ship, bridge to stern, is wrapped in bands of grav alternating in polarity. One will pull you down. The other will push you away. You should be alright to walk down the length of the hull as long as you don't move too fast across the field boundaries."

Acknowledgments all around.

I turn to Lenox. "Place your bucket wherever you think best between the drive plates and then catch up."

"Yes, sir." She's enthusiastic for getting to work.

"Let's go." I spin and lead the way again.

In the null g tunnel through the donuts, it takes just a few moments of effort before we're at the gaping mouth of the vessel's drive array. I fly over the lip, earning a close-up look at the thick layers of steel and composite materials that make up the hull. It's the material I'm hoping to breach with nearly a half-ton of TX.

I plant my feet on the hull's curve and turn just in time to see Silva alight right beside me with seemingly no effort at all.

"You're good at this."

"Of course." She's not bragging, just convinced.

Mostyn pushes her load up toward us. Below her, Lenox drifts out of sight into the concave array. As she disappears from view, she calls, "See you in a few, boss."

Mostyn's bundle rises above the edge, and Silva grabs a strap to pull it closer and settle it in beside us. Just as the bundle of metal buckets comes over the edge, it jerks out of her hands and shoots away like a balloon. "Dammit!" she curses.

I rocket off the surface as Mostyn apologizes over the comm for letting the explosives get away. It's my fuckup. I knew. I saw, but my variable-g intuition isn't plugged into all of my brain's circuits yet. Every time I hit my suit's auto-grav, my frontal cortex is tempted into laziness and wants to pretend it's back in earth's familiar constant field.

Graving way too hard for comfort, I reach the bundle when it's nearly thirty meters up. I grip the straps and pull hard to arrest its momentum. The buckets shift and the straps hum under the strain. I can barely hold the weight. I call to Brice. "Careful! We grav compensate our suits for the shift in field polarity and strength. These damn buckets aren't g-compensated at all."

"Don't worry about me," Brice answers, his voice straining as he wrestles with seven hundred pounds of TX trying to get away from him.

"Help him," I tell the others, as I try to control my load. It's harder than I guessed, and I'm not winning.

Over the comm, I hear the others grunting and pushing.

Realizing I don't have the strength in my hands to pull so much weight, I monkey climb around to the other side of the bundle, flatten my body, stiffen my suit, and use my suit's grav to drive and steer it.

"Back over the lip," Brice orders the other two.

"Inside the array?" pants Silva.

"Yes," Brice answers. "We need to handle this differently."

He's right. Crossing the hull in a two-g reversing field, each three-hundred-and-fifty-pound bundle with flip back and forth from seven hundred pounds down to seven hundred up. Not only will it be near impossible to move them, we'll be lucky if the buckets don't crush us in the attempt.

I push my load back toward the null field inside the drive array's concave expanse.

Chapter 34

One bucket at a time, nineteen buckets, five people, that's only four trips down the length of the hull. Simple math. Simple solutions when brute force isn't an option.

Walking up the cruiser's outer hull, I'm passing through an outward-pushing field, and my bucket's handle pulls me up with seventy pounds of pressure—a rigid balloon that after another ten steps will turn back into a heavy weight my tired fingers can barely carry.

The others are following me along the ship's dorsal crest, passing a row of railgun barrels, some with large diameters, some smaller, some long, others short.

"Where are we putting these?" asks Brice. He knows where, in the barrels of the guns. He's asking *which ones* we want to spike.

I point to a place I think is halfway down the length of the hull, slightly up the curve from where we are. "The ship's three fusion reactors are mounted inside the main hanger there."

"You want to take out the reactors?" asks Brice.

"Sounds good to me," adds Lenox, having placed her solitary bucket where she figured it would do the right kind of damage, grabbed another from our cache, and caught up with our line.

The field I'm walking through reverses, and the bucket swings down from above, nearly jerking my arm out of socket as it's pulled back toward the hull.

"God," says Silva. "This is tiring."

"It'll be worth it." I hope.

Mostyn, her voice taut from the strain, says, "These railguns, just ahead. Their barrels look wide enough."

"Yeah." No regular pattern exists in the distribution of gun barrel sizes protruding along the crest. Nevertheless, I've counted as we've been walking to gain an objective idea of how many barrels will suit our purpose, and to help me make the choice of where to start planting our bombs. It looks like we'll be able to place one bucket snugly inside a railgun once or twice every thirty feet. "We'll start with those, just ahead."

"Won't they just blow out through the barrel?" Mostyn's question is timid, but valid. "Will the explosions damage anything?"

"Of course," I tell her, going on to explain my hope, based on no engineering experience at all. "These barrels aren't built out of thick steel like the ones you see on the seagoing battleships in the old movies. They're designed to use gravity to push slugs down the long axis. All the support is in the rear." At least that's how I remember them from my look at the structures inside when we commandeered the Trog cruiser earlier. "The barrel isn't designed to contain the lateral pressures of a chemical explosion. Especially not this much chemical."

"So the gun breaches explode down inside the ship when the TX detonates?" asks Mostyn.

"Yes." I make it sound certain, although I don't know I'm right. Nevertheless, I've already figured out people like certainty when they're risking their lives. In fact, I suspect they prefer flawed certainty to faultless ambivalence. They might not admit to it in a discussion of hypotheticals over beers and brats in the backyard, but out in the shit with red-hot railgun slugs tearing through the air at six thousand miles an hour, they'd choose certainty every time.

"Twenty of these charges going off at the same time along this row of guns will do the trick." I scan back and forth, as I once more evaluate the layout. "The explosions will destroy the breaches on these guns and send a hail of shrapnel through the reactors inside. That'll kill the ship. With a bit of engineering luck, the detonation will blow this seam wide open. Either way, the ship is dead, no longer a threat to us."

"Except it's still full of Trogs," says Brice, pointing out the flaw in the plan. He's being a dick, because sometimes, I think it amuses him.

"Maybe we'll catch them with their pants down again." Another hope. Whether or not we kill any of their battle legions, we'll definitely kill all the Trogs unlucky enough to be in the ship's main hangar at boom time. The air inside will escape. They'll all suffocate."

Mostly I'm thinking, 'One step at a time. Let's kill the ship, and figure out how to deal with surviving Trogs afterward.'

I stop walking. I'm at the right place, I'm pretty sure, although with the curve of the hull, and me being so small and standing on such a large ship, I realize my perspective might be inaccurate. I don't say that out loud.

Brice, guessing my dilemma, points up. "You could take off and get a better view."

"You're kidding, right?"

He grins. "Of course."

Halfway down the ship's length, so close to the bow, to flex my suit's grav muscles and go zipping through space would surely catch the attention of the Grays on the bridge.

"Find a place for your charges," I tell them, as I step up next to a railgun barrel and slip my bucket inside. Not a perfect fit, but as close as I'm likely to get. I give the top of my bucket a nudge to slide it down to the bottom of the tube, and watch as it recedes into the darkness inside.

A little to my left, Silva is doing the same.

Brice, Lenox, and Mostyn are piling their buckets together into a large-caliber, ship-killing weapon pretty close to the one Silva is loading.

"That's a good idea," I tell them. "Concentrating our explosives over a smaller area will probably work better than spreading them out."

"Yeah," says Brice. "I know." As his tone conveys, I should have understood that he already knew that.

I think maybe he needs a shot of Suit Juice to take the grumpy edge off his fatigue.

Partially down the barrel, my bucket seems to be stuck. I have to use my rifle to tamp it in further. It doesn't go all the way to the bottom, I don't think, but there's no way to push any more. I sigh. Nothing goes as planned, even the little things.

Brice and the others, their explosives planted, are hustling toward the stern. Silva is standing by the railgun tube she loaded, and she's waiting on me.

I hurry along.

"Five down," she comms me over a private link, making it pretty obvious she was looking for any way to start a conversation.

"Yeah," I agree, suddenly at a loss for words that want to come so badly they burst full of nothing syllables. I've got nothing to fill a conversation with besides guilt, because the wife I promised myself to, a woman I loathe more than love, is shriveling away in my house back on earth. Worse yet, I'm not even sure how I short-circuited myself away from Silva's smile and down to the hag wrapped around my wife's sour soul.

The others are at least a hundred meters ahead of us and moving quickly.

I glance at Silva. "We should run."

She nods and sprints ahead, tumbles at the grav change, and catches her balance.

"I'll lead," I say, "I can see the gravity fluctuations."

Chapter 35

The distance from the aft drive array to the ship's midsection, crossing through dozens of polarity changes, and being jerked both up and down by the heavy buckets of TX has taken its toll. We've planted fifteen bombs. Four remain and we carry those with us. We're all bruised and tired, trudging forward to drop off our last load.

We're silent as we walk, nothing but labored breathing over the comm.

I wonder how Blair and her rebels are faring against the Trogs on the subterranean levels, and I entertain the foundationless hope that Blair has helped the rest of the troops from inside the warehouse to escape. I hope they're armed. I fantasize they've discovered the location where the Trogs have cached their automatic weapons. And I toss in the dream that Blair has organized them into units, eager for the coming fight.

Sadly, daydreams evaporate when luck in the real world changes polarity as quickly as a grav field.

"Trouble!" Lenox shouts over the comm.

I pull my eyes off my shuffling feet, scolding myself for inattentiveness as I scan for the source of the trouble, and I find it. A mob of Trogs is walking up the cruiser's curved hull from the starboard side. We're the reason they're coming.

Brice immediately drops to a knee, levels his weapon, and starts shooting. He's the only one who can fire his railgun, the only one not carrying a bucket.

Rounds veer up and down through the bands of gravity. Most hit the hull or fly off into space. The few that reach the widening wall of Trogs seem to be absorbed by the mass.

"This is shit!" curses Brice. "All these damn variable fields."

"We gotta get out of here," suggests Mostyn, not panicking. She's run her evaluation of the situation, come to a conclusion, and she wants it heard.

"We have to plant the rest of the TX," says Lenox, calmly.

All of those thoughts are running through my head already. I have to make a quick choice. Premiere on the list is whether Lenox is wrong, right, or committed blindly to my plan. Will that last hundred and fifty pounds of TX make the difference?

"Lenox, Silva, Mostyn," I say. "Plant those last buckets. Brice—"

He laughs because he knows what's coming, if not exactly, then he already has the idea. Brice stops his futile firing and taps furiously on his d-pad. "I'm transferring control of all the detonators to Lenox."

She's on her d-pad. "Got it."

"Plant those explosives," I command her. "Make your way clear of the ship and then blow 'em all."

I set my bucket on the hull. It's one that'll go unutilized.

"Move!" Lenox orders the girls.

Turning to Brice, I say, "Stay on my six. These grav fields will get pretty fucked up once the Grays see we're airborne."

I jump into the air and max grav right toward the center of the Trog line, weapon on full auto, a fiery stream of deadly metal blasting out in front of me.

Chapter 36

"Jesus!" shouts Brice. "There must be a thousand of 'em."

Seeing the immensity of the mob coming over the curve of the hull, I know Brice is right.

Spears of red sear past us as we fly. Trogs are shooting back. Most of them aren't, as I realize one of the reasons their preferred weapon is the disruptor. In variable-g, you never know where your railgun slugs will end up.

I veer to the right and claw for altitude, firing down on the Trogs from above, pulling their attention away from Lenox, Silva, and Mostyn, who are trudging along the cruiser's spine to make it to the location where they'll put these last bombs.

"Not too much altitude," Brice admonishes, as we pick up speed. "Or they'll fire the ship's guns at us."

The cruiser's gunners have no chance of hitting us at this range with the speed we're moving, yet he's right. If the gunners open their breeches to load their weapons, they'll find the explosives. I angle back toward the mob and see several black forms spring out of the mass and fly toward us. "Ghost Trogs!"

"Shit." Brice is looking. "Where?"

I point.

I cut a hard turn and angle for an empty swath of hull, well behind the advancing horde.

We cross a grav boundary, and I feel a punch that knocks the breath out of me. The grav is suddenly intense. I compensate as I shout a warning to Brice.

He hits the boundary and tumbles out of control.

It has to be four g's, at least.

Below me, as I careen toward the hull, I see Trogs falling over. The ratcheting grav field is fucking with them, too. At least there's that.

I hit the hull and roll. Trogs are all around me, on their knees and on their backs, reeling from the g.

Brice smashes down on a Trog, rolls, and springs up on wobbly knees, weapon firing.

The grav starts to ease and I bounce to my feet, leveling my weapon, pulling the trigger to clear a path in front of me. "This way," I shout, as I do my best to run.

The Trogs outside the field, ten meters away, are rushing toward us, stumbling as they encounter the change.

I amp up my grav again and take off. Good damn thing for us most Trogs like to keep their feet on the ground.

"Where'd those ghost Trogs go?" asks Brice urgently.

I glance at the black above us and see nothing. My bug can't find their mass. My grav sense is overwhelmed by the rapidly changing fields. I feel like I'm in a dark room with somebody strobing a flashlight into my eyes.

I spin to aim my weapon at the Trogs closing in around Brice, and fire at a handful from the side. "Get off the ground, Brice!"

He jumps as he works the grav control on his data pad. He's mobility-handicapped relative to me because he doesn't have a bug.

"This way!" I shout.

Brice flies toward me, and I'm heading for another empty space on the hull.

"Ghost!" he warns.

Instinctively, I tuck my head and roll as I go into a dive. A black blur with a bright blue blade soars past me, scaring a load into my suit's recycler.

"I never saw him." My mouth is on autopilot with out-loud thoughts.

"We need to get down," shouts Brice.

Looking back at the mob of Trogs, I see we're at least thirty meters past them and they're turning to come our way. Safe enough.

Brice is already angling for the hull, and his legs are starting to run even though he's not down yet.

I'm scanning and flying backwards, looking for the second ghost.

My feet touch down, and I spray a wide arc of slugs that veer toward the deck as the g fluxes again.

"Damn those Grays!" grunts Brice, as he flips his suit back to auto grav so he can concentrate on defending himself rather than managing grav changes.

His railgun spews out a stream of hot slugs.

To my right, I see the ghost Trog who'd just missed me with his blade. He's charging on foot.

I jump to my feet and sprint toward him, railgun blazing as I close the gap.

My rounds go up, down, and wide, but they pound his deflectors and knock him off balance. He falls as I cross the last few meters.

While he's trying to bring his disruptor around to cut through my neck, I push the barrel of my railgun under his outstretched arm, well inside his defensive grav, and send a handful of rounds through his suit, exploding out his back in a puff of shattered bone and blood.

No time to revel in my ghost Trog kill, I spin to see Brice swinging his disruptor in a fight with the other ghost, a towering, thick one, a giant among Trogs. "Get out!" I shout. "Get out of there!"

Brice ducks under the ghost Trog's blade, and jumps as his free hand moves to his d-pad's grav controls.

I jump too, and max grav directly at the ghost whose attention follows Brice into the air above his head.

At the last breath, I switch my power to defensive grav and smash bodily into the Trog.

He flies into a line of his simpleton brothers, and I angle up, slowing and spinning as I bring my weapon to bear, spraying the whole mess of them from above with un-aimed rounds, hoping for a hit.

"This way," shouts Brice.

"We can't hold this many," I tell him.

My God, I'm a deductive genius when it comes to the obvious!

"Of course we can't!" He angles toward the hull again, trying to move us another forty meters farther from the disorganized mob of Trogs.

He touches down, spins, and raises his rifle, ready to fight.

A second later, I plant my feet on the hull beside him, and start shooting as I comm the squad. "Lenox, we're pushing our luck here."

"Thirty more seconds," she tells me, "then get your ass out of there."

Chapter 37

The sky fills with fireflies of red zipping past us, some near, most far, railgun slugs fired by Trogs angry for having missed their chance to kill us when we were down among them.

Thirty seconds?

I didn't count the ticks.

Brice and me both empty our magazines and take off. With only disruptors left and no explosives, we have no defense against so many Trogs and only our lives to trade for a delay.

All we can do is try to keep their attention and hope a ghost Trog doesn't catch us. We're heading away from the Trog cruiser, back toward the asteroid where we picked up Lenox and the others.

"Silva, Mostyn, Lenox," I call. I hear only static.

"Lenox," calls Brice as the grav fields shrink to null around us.

No response for him either.

The mob of Trogs runs across the hull, looking every bit like an aquatic invertebrate preying on a fish.

I accelerate toward the asteroid's horizon, searching the surface as I fly, hoping to see the others.

"The ship's turning," says Brice.

I glance back to see the massive cruiser slowly rotate, bringing one of its spines of railguns to bear, but not the one we planted our explosives in. "Follow me!" I veer hard to the right.

Brice is close behind.

A volley of huge railgun slugs streaks past us and explodes on the asteroid's surface.

"That's overkill!" shouts Brice, like he's being treated unfairly. A bit uncharacteristic for him.

"I'd say they were pretty pissed about us being on their ship." I turn again, going up this time.

Railgun rounds start to pour out of the ship.

"Over the horizon!" shouts Brice. "We need the asteroid between us and them."

"Max grav!" I shout back. "As fast as you can go."

"I hope you're off the ship!" That catches my attention. It's Lenox on the comm.

I look back at the cruiser as I accelerate, not an entirely smart thing given how fast I'm moving with the asteroid below me and debris in the sky everywhere. I'm rewarded for my carelessness. The upper spine of the ship erupts in fire and shrapnel as railguns mounted there fly apart.

"Our TX!" I shout at Brice.

He turns to see.

All along the gun spine, the cruiser splits open, and the rent in the hull stretches wide as hunks of bent metal small and large blast into the vacuum. For a second, I can see clearly into the giant ship. Trogs inside are looking up at empty, black space, their death.

The cruiser lurches.

Another explosion rocks it.

Bodies and railgun slugs pour out through the gaping wound.

The grav fields flicker on and off, overlap, and stress the hull in places where it's now weak.

A huge section along one side of the tear caves in and is then pushed back out by escaping gases.

The ship starts to spin and bend.

Trogs that had been on the surface of the hull, the ones trying to kill us, are running in every direction. Some are making the most uncomfortable choice for a Trog and going airborne, leaping for the nearest asteroids.

Cracks spider-web across the hull and spread wide. Lights flicker. The grav fields go from chaotic to frenetic.

"This is going to get fucked up out here!" shouts Brice. The sky is filling with high-speed jetsam. It's impacting the asteroid below us, and flying past into deep space.

The grav fields near the center of the cruiser, where our bombs did the most damage, flash brilliant blue. I feel the sting all through the bug's tentacles in my brain as the ship rips apart—half rocketing away from us, two other massive hunks coming our way.

"Shit!" I over-grav my plates and burn for the asteroid's far side.

Brice sees the same situation as I do and does his best to keep up.

In moments, I'm down close to the surface on the backside, and I'm reversing my field to avoid a crushing impact. Thankfully, the familiar pop of frying plates doesn't sound. I've gambled again with my personal orange terrarium, and I'm alive.

My feet find dirt, and I switch to auto grav and start to run.

Brice touches down ahead of me, and I point to a ravine between two ragged ridges of stone.

"Catch me if you can!" he shouts as he finds his feet, switches to auto grav, and sprints.

The asteroid rumbles as part of the cruiser impacts on the other side. The ground beneath us shifts suddenly to the left and both Brice and I tumble down.

He's quicker to recover, and he's moving again.

I'm crawling and pushing with my grav and running as the star field above us races across the sky. Grav around us fluctuates wildly and the stone below us shakes like it's going to disintegrate.

Brice finds his way into the fissure first and turns to see me tumble over on top of him. We bounce off each other, and off the stone walls, as our mutual defensive grav fights with the asteroid's ambient field and wild fields flaring through everything around us.

I'm on my back, lying on jagged rock when I stop moving. Looking up, seeing the tiny sparkle of our sun slide across the sky, I know the asteroid is spinning. That thought barely has a moment to gel when the Trog cruiser's grav array fills the sky above and crashes into the rocks protecting us.

CHAPTER 38

I'm the first to poke my head through the gap of twisted steel and shredded hull composite, and notice the sky above is still moving. "I'm through."

Brice sighs his relief.

We've been working our way through the wreckage trapping us in the shallow canyon for nearly two hours.

"That was a hell of an impact," I tell Brice. "The asteroid is spinning pretty quickly."

"Can you make it all the way out?"

"I think." I wriggle myself through the hole, careful not to move too fast or push too hard. Plenty of sharp edges around me could tear a fatal hole in my thin orange sanctuary. If I get too anxious for freedom, it could be my death.

"I'll admit it," says Brice. "I wasn't a believer." He's talking about our plan to use Tarlow's TX to destroy the Trog cruiser.

I laugh. "Me neither. I was just placing a bet."

"Same here," Brice laughs, too.

Plenty of new metal meteors are in the sky racing away from us, remnants of the star-faring leviathan we killed.

I pull my legs up, turn, and sit on the edge of the hole. "I'm out."

I can't help but notice Jupiter's ragged stripes of rust and gray coming up over the horizon, engulfing our eastern sky. Pulling my boots free, I turn to reach a hand in to help Brice.

"Jesus," he says, as he pokes his head through the hole. "That's a sight." Then he grins because we're out of immediate danger. "I can't believe that worked."

I've had a lot of time to think about it while we were exploring the wreckage to find a way through. "Those ships are built for a specific kind of warfare, big ship-to-ship engagements. It's the kind of fight they expect to be in. The unofficial rules of their warfare. Doing things the way they've always done." I look down at Brice. "They're going to be rethinking a lot of that now that we've destroyed five."

"That worries me." Brice settles in for a moment, resting in the hole, the urgency gone now that he can see the sky. "We're winning because we keep surprising them. What happens when we run out of surprises?"

I laugh.

"What?"

"We're humans," I tell him. "We've been killing each other since the dawn of time, and coming up with new ways to do it at every turn. We'll never run out of fresh ideas. It's the genius of our species."

"I suppose you're right."

"Damn right, I'm right." I grin.

Brice laughs.

"The Grays and the Trogs and any other imperial dipshits in this galaxy better figure it out because they're dealing with humans now. We might not have the tech, but we have an irrepressible hankering to slaughter."

I guess, tired of my pontifications on warfare, Brice heaves himself out of the hole and looks up to see Jupiter reach its zenith, high-noon, filling half the sky above.

I realize, we can't be in the asteroid belt. In fact, the Potato never was. We're way too close to Jupiter.

I stand and straighten up to look around. "I'll bet we make a full day in ten minutes. Maybe forty-five."

"A day." Brice laughs as he sits on the edge of the hole with his feet dangling inside. "It's weird to think of it that way. A day is twenty-four hours on earth's rotation." He watches Jupiter barrel across our sky. "We're moving, too, right?"

He's right. We're not only spinning, but flying through space.

Brice scans the sky.

"You can't see it until the sun comes up."

"The Potato?" He asks.

"That's what you were looking for, right?"

"Yeah."

"Give it a minute."

"Are we pretty far?"

I nod.

"Really far?" he asks.

I nod again. "I saw it when I was still in the hole and first spotted the sky. It was a smudgy brown spot up above us then."

"Shit," he says. "A big, brown spot?" He's hopeful for the word, 'big.'

I shake my head, straighten my arm, and hold a finger against the sky. "The size of a penny maybe. A dime."

"How far do you reckon the asteroid is?"

I'm scrutinizing the tip of my finger. "Maybe it wasn't *that* big."

"You're not making me feel better."

I turn to look at him as Jupiter slides toward our horizon. "Is that what you wanted, me to make you feel better? Despite your off-color humor, I had you pegged for a no-bullshit kinda dude."

He sighs. "Sometimes the burden of the straight scoop wears me down. Maybe a little sugar-coating now and again wouldn't be a bad thing."

"I think they're sending a grav lift out to pick us up right now." I grin.

Brice grimaces. "Too much sugar."

"I know."

"What do you propose?"

I take a moment to examine my d-pad, looking for info on how much H I might still have in the tank. As usual. It tells me just about nothing.

"Looking to see if anyone is in comm range?" Brice looks at his d-pad.

"H," I tell him. "My suit burns it like it has a leak or something."

"It's these micro-reactors," Brice tells me. "The smaller they are, the less efficient."

"How are you set?" I reach around to my back and tap mine as if that's going to give me any information.

"That's pointless," Brice tells me.

"I know. My indicator doesn't work."

"There's a warning light built into your helmet display."

"The light doesn't do anything until I run completely out."

"That's not very convenient."

I reach down and check for the spare canister on my leg, only to realize I never obtained a spare after the last one ran dry. "That mining hut. The one Lenox said had all the spare canisters in it. We need to find it."

"This asteroid isn't that big." Brice looks back and forth across the rough landscape, then points. "They were drilling those cores down through the centerline. If we follow the line of holes, we'll come to that shack."

Brice is already out of our gopher hole and walking across the broken section of cruiser hull. He's not one to dick around once he makes up his mind. I follow, letting my suit's auto grav keep my feet oriented toward the asteroid's center of mass.

"So we stock up on H and cal packs," he says, "then what?"

Calories. I forgot about those. I can't remember the last time I ate something. I take a sip through my calorie tube, and nothing comes out. "Crap. I think my cal pack is dry, too."

"Should be plenty of both in that shack."

"Yeah."

We make our way slowly down to the surface, and I wonder as I plant my feet on the ground why we didn't just hop off and float down.

Jupiter is just starting to slip below the horizon when I say, "I think if we put on fresh H packs, we each load on a spare, and then grab a few more," I tap a few of the empty magnet mounts on my belt, "We should be able to fly back to the Potato on suit grav alone. I don't know. It can't be more than a few thousand miles."

Brice climbs over a tumble of rough stone and starts down the other side. "Back when I was working construction, there was this story about a guy whose lift went haywire or something. He'd just dropped his load on one of the rings." He's talking about the giant, ring-shaped station the crews were working to construct for the Grays. "This was back before my time, so who knows how much is true. You know how stories go over time. They get better."

I agree.

"They said the ring was already spinning then." Brice focuses forward as he talks. "Nobody's sure what happened to cause the accident. Maybe he didn't account for the spin. Maybe he was a new guy making new-guy mistakes. Long story short, the ring's billion tons of mass collides with his lift and mashes something in his grav accelerator mechanism. His ship shoots out of there like he's just floored it. I mean he took off faster than anybody had ever seen one of those lifts move."

"Yeah?" I make it over the tumble of stones and follow Brice as he seems to have a good bead on where we're headed.

"In no time, the grav lift shoots out of the orbital plain and disappears from view. Everybody figures the guy died in the collision."

I make the brilliant deduction the story has a kicker, so I keep my mouth quiet and wait for Brice to surprise me with it. I'm polite that way.

"What they learned later was this guy was knocked unconscious by the collision. He wakes up seven or eight hours into his flight. His ship is still accelerating away from earth, and he has no way to slow it down. So his choice is to sit there and wait to die, or do something."

That's my prompt. "What did he do?"

"He jumped out of the ship."

"He used suit grav to get himself back?" I ask.

"Yeah," answers Brice. "That's it exactly. Only he was smart enough to know he couldn't do a max grav burn or he'd use up all of his H and then suffocate. So he did a slow burn—a real slow burn—just enough to reverse his speed. Because he was in the ship, he was already moving away from the earth at twenty or thirty thousand miles an hour. He had to burn through all of that negative speed, get up a little forward speed, and then kill it. Then he had to hope he was going fast enough to make it back to earth before he ran out of H to sustain the suit. Go too fast, you burn too much H on acceleration. Go too slow, and you burn all your H on life support during the long trip back. He prayed he made the right guess on how long and how hard to burn. All he had then was hope."

"I take it the d-pads weren't sophisticated enough back in those days to make the calculations for him."

Brice shrugs. "Same d-pads we have now. Probably an older version of the software. It didn't matter. Half the time, his was on the fritz. He had to eyeball the whole thing. Course, acceleration, everything. Then he had to rest calmly in his suit using minimum energy so he could max his time to stay alive."

"I take it there's a happy ending."

"No." Brice shakes his head like that much was obvious from the start. "He died and froze to death on the way. Solid chunk of ice when they intercepted his body floating in earth orbit one day."

"How long was he out there?" I ask.

"Nearly two months before they found him," says Brice. "He recorded a diary on the d-pad. One of the only features still working. That's how they knew what happened to him."

"Why did you tell me this story?"

"Because if you're thinking, we're going to suit grav back to the Potato, I don't want to end up like a popsicle. Let's take plenty of H and plenty of C. Like all we can haul with us."

"Sounds like good advice."

CHAPTER 39

We arrive at the shack, the remains of it, anyway. It's been smashed. A gouge a hundred meters long runs across the ground and through its remains. Half the shack is just gone, ripped away, and who the hell knows where any of it is? The half still on the ground is crumpled flat.

Equipment that had been inside is broken and scattered, some on the surface, some floating. Other pieces drift slowly into space.

Brice, not fazed by the destruction, drops to his knees, and starts rifling through the debris. "Let's hope the Potato didn't take it this bad." He glances up at me with a silent request to affirm or rebut his hope for our soldiers back there.

I'm at a loss. If thoughts of the Potato's destruction have been bubbling through Brice's gray matter during our hike around this little rock, he's way ahead of me. I was too focused on our problems to think of them. Now, newbie to this set of fears, that they all might be dead, that the station might be destroyed, that the smudge of brownish-gray I saw in the distance might have suffered its own collision and might be careening so fast away from us we'll never catch it...

Oh, fuck it!

Any combination of a thousand terrible outcomes might have befallen bitchy Blair and the soldiers we left at the mining colony, and I don't know what to feel about any of that.

"You gonna help me?" Brice asks. "Or watch?"

"Watching is good."

"Yes, Major." Brice tugs at a sheet of metal once part of a flimsy wall.

I step over to help while I piece my composure together with the glue of our desperate situation. By all rights, we shouldn't have lived this long, and we shouldn't have any long-term aspirations in the realm of continued existence. Death is sure to wrap its bony fingers around our necks soon.

"Just kidding, man." I bend over and grab the piece of metal Brice is tugging at. Our combined strength is enough to yank it free.

Brice crawls inside the wreckage, and I heave the sheet of metal into space, sending it into orbit around the asteroid. When I turn back toward Brice, he's working through the jumbled mess, busy and quick, thankfully not desperate.

"H packs?" I ask, still working through my sudden dance with distress. "Any luck?"

"Looking." He shoves junked equipment and digs through the smaller pieces, creating a cloud of metal and other materials—all sizes, all weights.

I scan the area, looking for cartridges. Could they have all been blown off into space? I look across our rugged, curving landscape. I look in the sky. How far away could those little white bottles go and still be visible? Would a hundred meters be too far? Two hundred? And what about our rotation and translational velocity?

Deep breath.

I'm not prone to panic, yet I feel like I slipped on some kind of mental banana and I'm having trouble finding my feet.

"Jackpot!" Brice could have said 'hemorrhoid,' and if he'd said it with that much excitement, the syllables wouldn't have mattered. His tone told me what I needed so desperately to hear. He's found H.

"A lot of them?"

"A collapsed cabinet." He's up on his feet, legs bent, straining to drag something free. "A wire cage thing." He gasps with the effort. "Fifty, sixty bottles in here."

"H?" I ask, "Or C?"

"Both, looks like."

I'm beside him in a heartbeat, helping pull the deformed wire box free, looking at it with a love only someone who has starved or thirsted can understand.

"Looks like Trog stuff."

"H is H," I tell him. "Hydrogen has the same recipe everywhere."

Brice doesn't laugh.

I thought it was funny.

"Trog cal packs." Brice isn't happy about that. He steps backward, dragging the metal cage free.

"Can we use their cal packs?" I ask, concerned maybe their food might be poisonous to humans.

"Can." Brice straightens up and admires his work. "Tastes like grapefruit rind purée. Disgusting stuff. It'll keep you alive, though."

"Wonderful."

"And once you plug one into your suit," Brice grimaces, "that shit stays in your system and makes all your cal packs taste like shit for two or three months. The only way to get it out is to have the techs do an overhaul."

"I take it you've had it before."

Brice nods. "Back on Ceres. At the end, we were scavenging them off dead Trogs." Brice drops to his knees, then bends the cage's doorframe to open it up.

"You've had some experiences out here, haven't you?"

"Yeah, I suppose."

I sit down on a hunk of stone and stare up at Jupiter rising again over the asteroid's horizon. "When you came up, is any of this what you expected? I mean, I've seen some crazy shit, and it's only been a few days for me. I can't start to guess all you've been through."

Brice laughs with the giddiness of a man who just earned a long extension on life. "I gotta be honest, things are more interesting since you arrived."

"You mean space was just another boring version of earth?"

"No, nothing like that." Brice seats himself cross-legged beside his prize. "If you think these past few days are par for the course, they aren't. I think guys with lives this interesting don't tend to live long enough to tell their friends about it."

Still staring at Jupiter's red spot with fascination, I ask, "You were in construction at first, right? Why'd you come up? You had to know back then that life expectancy was short for construction workers up here."

"I did," says Brice as he pulls an H pack out of the crunched cabinet. He shakes it and listens, definitely a habit left over from his life back on earth. There's no way he can hear the liquid hydrogen splashing inside the bottle. That's when I get it. He can feel the hydrogen moving inside. He tosses the H to me.

I press a small button along the top edge of the bottle, and a band of green lights flashes bright to tell me it's full. That's a relief. I wrap the bottle in the Velcro straps on my right thigh and breathe a well-deserved sigh.

Brice is putting a full bottle on his thigh as well. "Feels good knowing you're going to live three more days. Right?"

I agree, of course. "It's a funny thing knowing your life expires as soon as that little bottle runs dry. I never thought about it when I was back on earth. I never thought about the details of life out here, how it was so different."

"You mean the null g?"

"No," I say, "everybody thinks about that. You know, when you're a kid and dreaming of coming into space, it's all about zero-g, and rockets blasting, and space battles with aliens. Stupid shit like that. No, I mean the details."

Brice laughs loudly. "We've done some of that, right? So you're not far off. But you're right, life out here isn't what you think it's going to be when you're sitting on the farm dreaming about rocketing into the void."

"Is that why you came up?" I dig. "To escape the farm?"

"Of course," says Brice. "Some people were made for Nebraska life, living in an endless sea of wheat, rolling hills to the horizon, peace and quiet under blue skies. My parents loved it. They were the right people for that kind of living. I hated it. At least I thought I did."

"So you weren't drafted into the construction crews, you volunteered?"

"I'm a genius like that."

Chapter 40

The mangled shelf containing the H and C packs turns out to be the best container we have available. With one of several carabiners attached to my suit's belt, I connect to one end of the shelf. Brice connects to the other. It'll make for awkward going, however, staying connected once we're out in the void will be worth any imposition.

We talk. We weigh the pros and cons. We do it quickly. We're both pragmatic. We both know the longer we stay on our spinning rock, the more likely we'll die.

And then we wait.

Jupiter sinks below the horizon, and the sun's tiny bright sparkle rises above the other.

"I don't see the Potato," says Brice, peering into the blackness.

"Give it a minute." I'm looking toward the horizon as well, trying to remember where we last saw the asteroid colony with respect to the position of the sun. I point to a spot in the sky. "Maybe around ten o'clock asteroid time." *I'm so clever.* "I think that's when we'll see it come up."

Brice looks. "When was the last time you *did* see it?"

"Before we started digging this shelf out of the collapsed shack."

"An hour?" Brice asks.

"Sure, I guess."

"How much farther away are we, do you think?"

I shrug. "I don't have any clue how fast we're moving."

We watch and wait as the sun climbs in our sky. I begin to think maybe I was wrong, and begin to wonder about other possibilities. Taking all I don't know about orbital mechanics into consideration, the possibilities of where my thinking and planning went wrong are too far beyond my educational level to even guess at.

Still, I scan the sky, trying to find that grayish-brown smudge of hope. "You know there's something I always wondered about?"

"What's that?" asks Brice, his eyes riveted to the sky.

"The people in Breckenridge, up near the spaceport—we had this image of farmers, like they always had plenty to eat because they had farms."

"Like Phil had plenty to eat?"

"We talked about Phil's problem."

"Sorry," says Brice. "I couldn't help myself."

"That's okay. I know you don't like him."

Brice takes a moment before putting together a real response. "You know the MSS has an office in every farm county, right?"

"I didn't know that, exactly." It makes sense, though. "Phil's wife, remember her?"

Brice's smile looks a little too lascivious.

I'm pretty sure it's a dig at me for my indiscretions. "Sydney, she worked as an auditor for the Farm Bureau. MSS, right?"

"They have to be in charge of every detail." Brice scans the heavens for a few more silent moments. "When I was a kid, there was this family that lived out east of town. I didn't know them well. I saw the kid in school. He was a few grades ahead of me and kind of a bully. A chunky kid. Phil reminds me of him a little bit."

"Because he was chunky?" I guess.

"Maybe," admits Brice. "Not a lot of people around who can afford the luxury of a few extra pounds."

Truer by the day on an earth ruled by twiggy Gray bastards.

"What happened to the kid?" I ask.

"I was pretty young. Maybe second grade, so I didn't really understand it. The MSS arrested the kid's family, him, his two sisters, and the parents. Hung them all from some gallows they had the farmers build on the lawn in front of the courthouse. Said they were hoarders."

"Food hoarders?" I'm angered, but not surprised. It's a common story. It seems anytime the MSS is too lazy to beat the hell out of someone, they have them hanged instead.

"I didn't understand what that meant," says Brice. "'Hoarders' is all everyone called them after that. The MSS officer stood them on dining room chairs under a beam with nooses on their necks. He screamed at them for a long time, you know the way they do, all red-faced and spit dribbling. When he ran out of breath, another one walked down the line and knocked the chairs out from under their feet. They kicked and wiggled while their faces twisted and turned purple and their eyes bulged out. It gave me nightmares."

"Why do you think your parents made you watch?"

"Everybody in town had to be there," answers Brice. "That's the way the MSS wanted it. You know how they are."

"Yeah." I've got nothing but dark thoughts for those fuckers.

Brice looks up at the sun and then scans across the horizon again. "Should we see it by now?"

I nod, but don't say anything.

"After that," says Brice. "No more chunky kids in school. As a matter of fact, I never saw another overweight person who wasn't MSS until I met Phil."

"Yeah, the MSS is never short on food."

Brice points at the sky. "I think we waited too long." He turns to look at the H and C packs in the deformed cage linking us together.

I extend an arm and point it at the sun. I jab another downward, in the direction I think Jupiter is currently orbiting. Rotating one arm around to point at nothing apparent, I say, "The Potato should be that way. We can't see it because it's small and doesn't reflect any light."

"What does your bug say?"

"I wish something more. I'm sensing masses all through the darkness out there. Probably pieces of the ship. Maybe other asteroids."

Brice laughs. "Are you saying we head out in that direction and pray we run into it?"

I pat the wire cage holding our provisions. "We have enough hydro to last us for months, so we can stay here and hope somebody happens upon us, or we can go. The longer we wait, the less likely we are to find the Potato."

"I'm not sure we're at all likely to find it now."

Looking into the blackness for any hint as to the location of the asteroid, I admit, "You're right, but we both know that staying is choosing to die." I look around. "Though we will miss out on all the modern conveniences and great views."

"I'm not arguing." Brice sighs. "I don't want to spend the last weeks of my life picking out the best hole for you to bury me in. Better to take our chances out there."

I look up at the stars to find my bearings. "I think I know the direction. If you want to relax, I'll handle the grav in both suits."

"Fine by me. Just say the word."

"Hold onto the cage," I tell him. "For stability. No point in putting all of our trust in me or that carabiner." I gently apply the grav, and we lift off the asteroid's surface. "I'll accelerate for thirty minutes or so, and then we'll coast and see what we see."

"You're the pilot."

Chapter 41

The only gauge I have for our speed is the rapidity with which the asteroid we left shrinks behind us, and that tells me just about nothing. We might be moving at two hundred miles an hour or five thousand.

And direction?

What the hell was I even thinking when I jumped off our rocky little home trying to eyeball-navigate across the solar system? The smaller that asteroid shrinks, the more folly this seems.

Sure, Jupiter is behind me. The sun is to my left. Brice and I are streaking toward the asteroid belt, going pretty much in the direction of the Potato, but I know that if the asteroid is a little farther away than I hoped, if we're a few degrees off, we might zip on past it, missing it by fifty or a hundred thousand miles and never know.

Maybe that's the worst part, I don't know how far away we were when we started, and I don't know how close we need to be to see it. Maybe every part is the worst part, right down to staying put on the asteroid and waiting to die.

"They left them there," says Brice.

I look back at him. "What are we talking about?"

"Those people they hanged."

I chuckle, and then apologize. "I'm not laughing about the hoarders. I just didn't know we were still having that conversation."

"Better than staring at the black and thinking about what dying out here will feel like. Nothing to touch. No grav. No heat or cold. Nothing to feel at all. How long before you think a person would go insane out here?"

I don't want to talk about any of that, so I change back to the subject Brice was hoping to keep his mind busy with. "How long did the MSS leave them hanging in front of the courthouse?"

"Months," he answers. "Birds would sit on them and pick at their skin. Coyotes came around at night and chewed at their feet. We didn't come into town but maybe once a week, sometimes twice a month. There was less and less of them each trip. Then they just disappeared. Nothing left but ragged ropes and dark spots in the grass. At least the spots went away in the spring when the green grass grew in."

"The MSS left the ropes and the gallows there?"

"Might still be there," says Brice. "They wanted the farmers to know they were serious about food theft."

"Did it work?" I ask. "Or did people just hide it better?"

"That's an odd question."

"How so?" It doesn't seem odd to me. "We've all lived under the North Korean tyranny. We've all broken the law. Everybody becomes good at it, right? At least the ones of us who stayed alive."

"You sound like my dad."

"I think you and I are about the same age." I look him up and down. "Don't pull that dad shit with me." I smile.

"The summer after the hanging," says Brice, sounding particularly guilty, "I pilfered some corn from the harvest. I stashed it in the barn, back in the loft, a couple of bushels. It was enough so I'd be able to sneak in every day or so and eat some. I was always hungry."

"You got away with it." An easy deduction since I see Brice has lived to experience the good fortune of our current situation. "No big deal, right?"

Brice disagrees.

I decide at that moment all of his stories must have shitty endings.

"My dad followed me into the barn one day and caught me."

"What'd he do?"

"He beat the hell out of me."

Trying for some happiness in it, I say, "He was looking out for you."

"Not in the way you think," says Brice. "When he was done, he didn't take the corn. He didn't tell me to turn it in. He told me to get better at hiding it. If he could find it, so could the MSS. Then he went back to the house and left me in the barn."

"What'd you do?"

"I didn't know where to put it. I thought I'd already found the best place. So I fed it to the pigs."

"And you went hungry?"

"Nothing new for us," says Brice. "I didn't want my parents hanged in the square. So, like everybody I knew, I grew up starving surrounded by piles of food. I was kicked out of school after sixth grade like everybody else, and I went to work on the farm, twelve hours a day. By the time I turned seventeen, the Grays were siphoning every able body they could fit into an orange suit, and sending them to build that goddamn stupid giant wheel in space, floating forever at LaGrange Point One. When finished, it would have been a thousand miles across, three hundred wide. There were supposed to be two million square miles of happy Gray habitat inside when we were done. After that, the Grays were supposed to leave us alone on earth. They'd have their place, and we'd have ours. All that work for all those years. All those lives. You can't even measure it. And it was the first goddamn thing the Trogs destroyed when they attacked."

"Second." That just slipped out.

"Yeah," admits Brice. "They did attack the moon colonies first, yet the moon survived. We still own that."

Feeling my political hackles rise, I ask, "Nobody really believed the Grays would stop at one ring, did they? If we'd ever finished that one, they'd have made us build another and another and another. We're their slaves, and as long as they're alive in this solar system, it's always going to be that way."

"I don't need to hear your rebel recruitment pitch," Brice grouses. "Look at me, I'm already sold. I fragged my company captain. I'm complicit in a mutiny. I'm a rebel, and now I'll always be, whether I like it or not. I'm committed."

"Sorry." Not about Brice's choice to come to my side, but for me slipping a foot onto my favorite soapbox. "Sometimes it just happens. I hate the Grays even more than I hate the Trogs."

"Turns out they're the same people," laughs Brice. "Same management, anyway."

"Yeah." Looking for something else to talk about, I try another subject. "Did you like working in space?"

"At first, yeah, of course." Brice sounds suddenly nostalgic. "There's the novelty of it. Who wouldn't love it? Working construction in space is a lot harder than you think it should be. You still sweat. Sometimes so much you think you're going to die of heat stroke, or you freeze for days on end because you're suit's thermostat won't calibrate right. Or it gets the O_2 mix wrong, and you run around high as a kite, or your cal mix runs lean, and you lose twenty pounds over your three-week in-suit rotation, and you don't even know it because you never see yourself in the mirror, never step on a scale. You never even put on pants and figure out they're loose, because you're in the suit for the weeks-long stretch."

"Was that the deal?" I ask. "Three weeks in, and what, three days off?"

"Five off," says Brice. "The Grays were generous with us up there. You could get to the moon a couple of times a year, back to earth once every twelve months or so. If you were lucky. Mostly we spent our time off in the dorms on the site. Slums really, with stacks of bunks ten tall in warehouses for a thousand off-duty slugs just like you. Sounds shitty, and it was, but it was something. You were out of your suit. You could eat real food, for a couple of days anyway, before you were back on the colon cleanse to empty your system and prep for being back in the suit. At least you had artificial gravity and had a chance to feel another human's touch."

"Sounds like there's more to it than just that," I observe.

"There was a girl," admits Brice. "I was young. She was, too." He laughs. "Of course, there was a girl."

I chuckle because I'm a guy and I know, the girl always comes up. "Pretty?"

"You bet," says Brice. He laughs some more. "With every day that goes by, the girls in your memory grow prettier, or they turn meaner."

"Or both."

Brice finds that exceptionally funny.

I think of how Claire's flaws seemed to have evaporated in the years after she took in the hatchling, not in real life, but in my memory. In my mind, the real Claire died the day she embraced that Gray, and the woman I married was replaced by a withering facsimile.

I wonder whether she's still alive.

I feel suddenly like I've been away from the earth for months, yet I know it's only been days.

CHAPTER 42

"They organize the work crews into pods of six," says Brice. "Like the Grays do with things, everything is six-this and six-that. Six pods of six workers made up a crew. She was in another pod in my crew, all on the same rotation. I don't even remember how we met. I think we bumped into each other in a chow line on one of our five-day breaks. She talked about going to the moon because she'd never been. Neither had I. We were both new then. She started sending me messages when we were out in the void, and we started hooking up during our downtime. We explored the ring we were building. Hundreds and hundreds of miles of it were finished by then. Lots more were in some state of completion. We used to sit out on the framework of an unfinished section and look at all the orange suits crawling over the structure, millions of ants busy at work with countless shuttles coming and going, dumping materials brought up from earth. It was mesmerizing. Eventually, we grew comfortable with silence. We often sat with our legs dangling over a trillion miles of nothing, thinking what-if thoughts, and watching the universe slide by.

"We messaged a lot when we were on duty. We slept together during our rotations back to the slum. Funny thing is, by that time, I'd had my fill of space and so had she. We dreamed about going back to earth when our ten-year term was up. We talked about maybe getting a farm, can you believe it? At the time, we still believed once the stations were finished, life would be better on earth. We'd raise some kids, listen to the birds tweet, sit in the shade of a tree—a tree—you wouldn't believe how much you miss trees once the shine wears off the whole space thing.

"Maybe we'd go rogue, run up to Canada, hide in the mountains off the grid, and wait for all the shit to blow over." Brice's unexpected laugh comes out mean and hard, and I can feel he's carrying a lot of bitterness. I dread where the story is heading.

"We just wanted to be together in love," he continues, "and not have to hide in silence between the blankets of a single bunk with a hundred other workers in earshot, half of them knowing what you're up to and wanking to the sounds they can hear. It's perverse, but it's life up there. You get three weeks of isolation in your suit with only the sound of each other's voices to make you feel human, or you get five days of zero privacy.

"It's easy to get used to it because you realize every day you have less value than you *thought* you had the day before. You're a commodity, one of a billion copies from a planet that keeps making more just like you. The lifts keep bringing new ones up from the surface and hauling empty suits back down."

"The dead?" I guess.

"People die all the time," confirms Brice. "Anything will do it—space trash, accident, inadequate shielding. If you get lucky, if you get good, and you spend enough time out there, the solar radiation eats you up. You're brain goes first. You make mistakes. You get stupid. Your coordination goes to shit.

"The trick to staying alive is being picky about where you work. I learned that early on. If they were sending rivet teams inside or outside, you always took inside. You didn't have much shielding there, but you got a little, and over time, it makes a difference. Think of it like being an albino on earth and always avoiding the sun. It was kinda like that. You always wanted the thickest walls of whatever between you and the void. However, you can't do it forever. Hell, we were building a giant fucking donut in space. You couldn't avoid the outside.

"Worse thing, solar radiation is insidious. You don't know which are your high-risk days. It doesn't care, it kills you just the same."

Brice stops talking, and we float along in silence for ten, maybe twenty minutes before he picks the story up again. "I first noticed she developed a stutter. It happened occasionally, but enough. I tried to do what I could to have her rotated back to earth, inside workstations, something. She wouldn't have it. She was a real daredevil. She came to space for the thrill. She always took the most dangerous jobs.

"Maybe six months after the stutter became worse, she was in the wrong place when a newbie lift driver was bringing in a load of fill-dirt from moon-side. She saw it at the last moment. Well, maybe she missed the last moment by two or three. By the time she did see it coming, it was too late for her to dodge out of the way."

The next part is hard for Brice to say. I think he still loves her. "It was the kind of crash that looked like it should have killed her. That would have been a mercy on all of us." Brice pauses again. I'm not sure if he's silently crying or suffering while trying not to. "What we did to that driver... We didn't kill him. Maybe. I don't know. We beat the fuck out of him three times over. When we stopped, you couldn't see anything but blood inside his faceplate. He wasn't responding, but his d-pad said he was alive. Somebody gave him a shove and sent him off into space. Last we saw of him.

"My girl, she had one leg crushed halfway up the thigh, the other halfway down the shin. Her suit never punctured, so she avoided the mercy of a quick death. Her legs though, were beyond repair. Everybody saw that. They were like jelly inside her suit. We knew death would come for her, if not in a few minutes, then by the end of the day, whatever the hell that means in space where the sun shines all the fucking unmerciful time. Our MSS supervisor had her put in the discard bin."

"Discard bin?" I've never heard of that before.

Brice's mean laugh comes back, and I realize it's a kind of protection he armors his heart with when the shit of life weighs too heavy on his memories. "It's a warehouse, a garbage bin, literally, for people who are expected to die. The MSS doesn't waste infirmary beds on the terminal cases, and they don't want them taking up a bunk in the slum, sucking up real food and bringing down morale. Morale? What a fucking joke.

"Problem is, she didn't die. She suffered in the discard bin for weeks, stealing cal packs and H from others the MSS tossed in who eventually died. Why gangrene or blood loss or shock didn't kill her, no one knows.

"The MSS finally fished her out of the discard bin, sent her back to earth, and paraded her as a hero in the propaganda vids to demonstrate the courage of the orange suits serving humanity's partnership with our Gray brothers.

"It twisted her rotten inside.

"Our relationship didn't end, so much as sublimate into the vacuum, until one day it didn't bother me at all that I hadn't heard from her in weeks, and in fact dreaded the next message. It never came.

"We, us, whatever mythical thing people conjure in their minds to make themselves believe the bond of their infatuation is more than just chemical needs and engorged erections, that died. It suffered long and slow, just like her. In the end, it was a relief.

"Some time later, I earned a favor from an MSS supervisor with a kink for strapping young Americans. She took a liking too me." Brice laughs again, and this time it's the familiar voice of his dark soul I hear. "She rode me like a man-whore and I didn't care. She eventually grew tired of me, and called in a favor to have me invited to join the SDF. I ended up in the moon garrison, which was great—fucking great—until the war started."

Chapter 43

Two days zipping through the void, though for all I can tell, we might as well have been drifting in the same spot. The sun still shines harsh and unforgiving, anchored to its throne at the center of the solar system. Jupiter still dominates the sky behind us. Our position relative to both of them seems not to have changed. Only the absence of the little asteroid we escaped from gives us any hint that we moved.

Or did our acceleration away from the asteroid only serve to negate the speed we'd built up moving in the other direction? We have no navigational equipment, no way to gauge our speed against any of a dozen easily visible objects in the sky, all of which are so far from us and so large we'll never know whether we're moving or not.

"I've accepted it," says Brice after hours of silence.

"What's that?" I ask as I scan the sky in front of us, confounded by the disappearance of our gray-brown smudge.

"Death."

"You're giving up?" I ask curiously.

"No."

I turn to look at him. It's a nice change for my straining eyes. "What do you mean?"

"I'm not okay with it," he tells me. "I'm not quitting. I'm not going to cry and whine. That's all I'm saying."

"I'm not sure I see the difference."

"Sure you do," he argues. "It's how I face every fight with those Neanderthal Trog bastards, I accept I'm already dead. It makes the rest easy. You don't panic. You don't try to save your ass at the expense of anyone's life. You do your job. This ridiculous flying field trip through the solar system is like that. I just had to accept it."

"Huh." I laugh as I try to figure out my thinking on the subject. "I'm not sure I do the same. I think I wear a cloak of invincibility. It's a lie. I know it is. A useful lie."

"I'm going to make you an offer," says Brice, deeply serious.

"This already sounds bad."

He hesitates, and then starts. "We may have enough H here to last a month, maybe two. Hell, maybe a year. I don't know. What I do know is it'll last one of us twice as long as both of us."

"Hero suicide shit?" I don't believe it, and my surprise is obvious in my tone.

"No," Brice tells me. "I think finding a safe place for us to land our feet is a one-in-a-billion shot. I'm offering to give you my lottery ticket and double your chances. All I have to do is disconnect from this beat-up wire cage and zip off toward Jupiter. All the hydro is yours."

"Two times zero is still zero," I argue. "If I'm going to die, then I'd rather spend the rest of my time with someone to talk to. Twice as much time by myself sounds like a shitty trade." I catch myself. "Wait, you're not expecting me to make the same offer, are you?"

"No," Brice laughs. "You're the invincible one, right? I'm the dead one."

I laugh, too, and decide staring at the black sky is something I need a break from. I reorient myself so I can watch Jupiter imperceptibly recede behind us. "It's a beautiful view when you look this way."

Brice turns himself around. "I'm tired of looking at fucking stars anyway."

"I wonder how far we are."

"Maybe ask somebody when we get back to the Potato."

"Yeah," I chuckle. "I'll do that." I spot one of Jupiter's moons, tiny and crisp, a perfect sphere hanging in the sky as it slowly spins through its orbit. "Look, you can see Ganymede, I think." I point. "Right there."

"Yeah," says Brice, a smile in his voice. "I see it." He points, too. "Look, down there. Another one."

"Yeah." I see it, different in color, a bit smaller in diameter.

"How many moons does Jupiter have?"

"Sixty some, I think."

"That many?" Brice muses. "Almost hard to believe."

We both watch the Jovian giant for a while, pointing out moons as we find them orbiting slowly over the swirling surface.

"Look at that one," says Brice, pointing. "Just above that rusty band, in the gray."

"Where?"

"See the big spot?"

"Yeah."

"Follow the rusty stripe below it to the left, back, almost to the horizon."

I see it, but it's not well-defined. "I don't think that's—"

I can't believe it.

"What?" Not understanding the cause for my surprise, Brice is ready to pounce.

"I think that's the Potato."

"No." Brice is leaning forward. Habit.

I am too. I'm squinting. Anything to help. "It's got to be. We must have passed it. Shit. We must have missed it yesterday, or a few hours after we left."

"If that's it," says Brice, "I think we didn't start off on the right vector."

He might be right. He might not be. He might be accusing me. He might not. I don't care. "We have a bunch of H here. I say we burn through some bottles and speed this kiddy ride up. I'm tired of drifting."

"Spark it, buddy. Let's go home."

Chapter 44

Eight hours. Six canisters of H burned dry. I accelerated hard, guessed at a midpoint, and decelerated just as hard. We were nearly obliterated a dozen times by high-speed collisions with bits of stone and metal expanding in a deadly plume out from battles around the Potato's dirty smudge.

As harrowing as those close calls were, Brice and I are in good spirits, the best since we first rocketed away from the small asteroid we were marooned on. The Potato, still engulfed in a haze of dust with untold numbers of Trogs on the surface and in the subterranean complex, looks like an oasis to us.

I make a guess. "Less than a hundred miles, I'll bet."

"Do we have a plan?" asks Brice.

I chuckle, maybe from fatigue. I know I've slept in the past few days of our journey. I'm not sure how much. It's easy to lose track of your anchors in time and place when you're drifting in the void. "Since we started our burn, I've been pretty focused on driving." Translated as 'avoiding skewering space trash.'

Misunderstanding my weariness for irritation, Brice apologizes.

Our relationship is evolving. We're learning how to bicker our way around our moods.

"Sorry," I tell him. "I'm just tired."

"Might be a good time for a shot."

"Suit Juice?"

"Gift of the gods." Brice laughs lazily. "I don't know what's down there," he points at the Potato. "My bet is we'll wish we still had some ammo for these guns when we arrive."

"Shit. I forgot I was empty."

"There was that thing on the cruiser we blew up," says Brice. "Remember all the Trogs chasing us?" He laughs because I think he's tired, and in his exhausted brain, that seems like genuine hilarity.

Brice exhales loudly like he's just had a very satisfying orgasm.

I glance over at him. "What are you doing?"

He smiles and shows me his d-pad. "I just juiced."

"I thought you said the high dissipates the more you do it."

"I don't do it that often. Just enough." He nods toward my d-pad. "Give yourself a kick. You're gonna need it, and you know I'm right."

Yes, I'm sure he is. I hit the button on my wrist and feel the instant chemical love of lying molecules telling my senses I'm not a beat-down, butt-dragging draftee, but a born-again, electric-fueled, fusion-drive, ready-to-rock motherfucking killer.

Brice laughs at me.

I bust a belly laugh, too. "I love this shit."

"Love what shit?"

I laugh even harder. "You sound just like Penny when you do that."

"That wasn't me." Brice is serious. He's looking around.

"That's because it was me," says Penny.

I can't believe it. I'm scanning the sky, too. Is Suit Juice a hallucinogen? "You're alive?"

"Why wouldn't I be?" asks Penny.

"And Phil?" If she's alive, then his irritating, stupid ass must be, too. "The ship?"

"We're maybe ten klicks behind you," says Phil.

"Phil?" Brice's rapid improvement in fortune makes him sound happy even with Phil's name on his lips.

I spin around, and though I can just make out the Rusty Turd against the darkness, my bug sees its mass as clear as day. "I don't understand." Stuck somewhere in the purgatory of not being sure Phil was dead, I suddenly feel overwhelmed with relief he's not. Despite all the shit between us, all of his annoying foibles and his disgustingly enviable talents, he's the friend who's been beside me my whole life, my brother in every way except for the difference in birth-parents.

Phil says, "Gravitationally speaking, you've been glowing like a comet out here all day. I'd have to be blind not to see you. We'll pick you up. Once you're onboard, we'll talk."

Chapter 45

I'm not good with reunions and gushing emotions, but we hug—me and Penny, me and Phil, even Brice who's been burdened with my non-stop company for the past three days can't help but squeeze me like he never wants to let me go. Jablonsky smiles and gives me a perfunctory squeeze, which is satisfactory for both of us.

Lenox, Silva, and Mostyn, inexplicably on board all share in the warmth, Silva in particular. Our embrace followed by a lingering look into one another's eyes feels like something that should be shared by two people way more intimate than us. Nevertheless, it's not awkward, not one second of it.

It all lasts too long. Emotions bubble all over the comm, leaving smiles behind faceplates, and real human touch behind layers of worn orange composite and grav plates.

It'll do.

With our commando squad listening in, Brice shares our story with the bridge crew, the only three people on the Rusty Turd when the Trog cruiser popped out of bubble jump nearly on top of them. They listen, ask questions, and then explain to us how the cruiser's grav field bumped our ship like a billiard ball with such sudden force all three were knocked unconscious, and like Brice and I, they woke up shooting through space, thirty thousand miles from nowhere trying to understand what happened.

The ship suffered some damage they had to repair before they could get underway again. When they were finished and found their way back to the Potato, they saw the remnants my commando club left in their wake. Not knowing what had happened, not knowing the situation down on the surface, except that Phil sensed the presence of thousands of Trogs down there, they surveyed the outer asteroids while hailing on all the SDF frequencies. That's how they found Lenox, Silva, and Mostyn.

After that, they waited.

"We've been out here in space, a few thousand miles off the surface," says Phil, glancing at Jablonsky. "We're able to communicate with Blair, though we lose the signal at least half the time."

Jablonsky adds, "It's improving as the dust settles. Better by the hour, almost."

"We were trying to decide what to do," says Penny. "Unfortunately, Blair's not as forthcoming with information as she could be and she's not open to suggestions." Her eyes fall on Phil. "He has an idea."

I turn to Phil. "Which is?"

"Oh," interrupts Penny, needing to get one more word in, "Jill is back."

More good news? It's like real Christmas, the kind in the old vids where the kids receive so many great gifts they lose themselves in the wrapping paper pile. She says, "They shoved the other Trog cruiser into orbit around Jupiter and right now they're eight or nine thousand klicks away on the other side of the Potato."

"Her ship?" I ask, meaning the mining tug she and her platoon flew out with. "Her crew?"

"Fine and fine," Penny answers. "All safe. No casualties. Nothing happened along the way. Pretty boring trip."

Nodding, I'm mentally cataloging the pieces of my tiny military force. Where twenty minutes ago, it was Brice and me with no ammo deorbiting blindly onto a rock full of hostile Neanderthals, now I have a battle-tested fighting force, small, but effective.

"What's the story down on the Potato?" I'm already guessing it's not good, an easy leap given neither of my ships has chosen to land. *Clever General Kane rides again!*

"It's that insufferable Blair making a mess of everything," Phil blurts. "If she'd stop being so controlling—"

"This is not news," I tell Phil, slipping right into the snippy tone I generally take with him, one made comfortable out of habit.

Phil follows the pattern of our well-rehearsed behavior and starts to sulk.

Penny kicks me.

I feel like an asshole. "Sorry, Phil. You know I don't mean anything by it."

"Maybe if you treat me like you respected me," he responds, "it would be easier than apologizing after Penny forces you to."

"Phil," I'm trying for max sincerity. "I'm sorry. And thank you for saving our lives. In case that didn't come across earlier."

"Well not exactly," Brice corrects. "We mostly saved ourselves. The Potato is right over there."

Eye rolls. It's like we're a family.

I ask, "What's going on with Blair and our people down there?"

Phil turns to Penny. "I'll let her tell it. She's good with the succinct summaries you like."

I nod a thank you to Phil.

"Blair has nearly a hundred soldiers on sublevel three," Penny tells me. "They have some automatic weapons, and a cache of industrial explosives."

"Tarlow," mutters Brice. "He must have hauled some back down to the control center."

"That's where they are," says Penny, "in some control center, they have the whole level, mostly. It's contested. The

Trogs keep attacking. Our troops push them back but don't have the strength to press a counter attack. The Trogs aren't able to make gains, the soldiers can't escape."

"The prisoners down on sub nine?" I ask.

"Still there."

"Trogs?" That's the unanswered question that'll have the biggest impact on how I choose to proceed. "Do we have a solid estimate of how many Trogs made it down to the Potato?"

"Altogether," Penny pauses, because she sees the importance I'm attaching to the number. "Nearly six thousand."

"Shit." Brice beats me to the exclamation.

"Shit." I can't help but agree with him.

CHAPTER 46

Time for a poor leadership move. "I'll be honest with you." I look around at each of them on the bridge. "I don't know what to do here."

"I have an idea for a way to attack," says Phil.

Being careful with my tone, I raise an open hand to silence him first. "Before we talk about how we'll fight those Trogs, we need to decide *if* we should attack at all."

"If we should?" Phil isn't sure how to feel about that.

Penny leans back in her chair. "I just assumed."

"Six thousand," mutters Brice. He knows what hordes of Trogs can do. "It may be a stalemate down on sub three right now—it won't last. The Trogs have done this before, pretty much on every installation they've taken. If they can overwhelm with numbers, they do. In the narrow halls, like down in the sublevels, they can't mass and surround our smaller units. The battles drag out, for weeks or months. Attrition is a decisive factor. Supply is, too. Both of those are in the Trogs' favor. Eventually, Blair will have to watch all hundred of her troops die, or pray the Trogs decide to start taking prisoners again."

"We have to do something." Penny straightens up in her chair. "If we don't, if Blair dies, then we all do, too, right? Her kill switch will trip when her coal-clod heart stops beating, and then we're all gone." Penny tries to snap her fingers through her suit. It looks awkward, and if it made a sound, it wouldn't carry in the vacuum anyway.

"Not necessarily." Phil slips right into his knowledge-authority voice. He's about to enlighten us all, and he looks at me to make sure I'm paying close attention. "If we're out of range of her tactical comm when she dies, the kill switch won't affect us."

Penny runs a fast deduction. "So as long as we make a point never to come back here—"

"No," Phil interrupts. "Once her hydro pack runs dry, and her micro-reactor shuts down, her suit won't send the signal, ever. The kill-switch problem is solved for all of us."

I'm tempted by Phil's suggestion for solving the Blair problem. Luckily my mouth follows my heart more than the logic centers in my brain. "Condemning a hundred soldiers to die is something I can't do, not on the basis of this one factor. We need to set this idea aside for a moment."

"How can we set it aside?" asks Brice.

"Not possible," agrees Penny. "We're human."

"Fine." I sigh. "Do we have a moral obligation to try and save those people down there? Do we have a higher obligation to not throw our lives away on a lost cause? I think those are the most important questions we need to answer. And even if we choose to go in, can it be done? How do we have a chance against six thousand Trogs?"

"Phil has an idea," Penny reminds me, sounding irritated because I haven't yet let him air it. "You should listen."

I turn to Phil. We all do.

Phil smiles, because he has our attention. "We don't need to kill six thousand Trogs to win. If we're going with the theory the Grays are in charge and from everything I've heard from Blair, from everything we've learned so far, that's what it looks like to me. So, it's those six Grays we go after. If we capture them, we can make those legions of Trogs do anything we want."

"How sure are you about that?" asks Brice.

"Mostly."

"Brice." Penny puts a hand on his arm. "You know that's a crappy question. Phil will never be as sure as you'll want him to be. You two are both too different to ever come to common ground on that question, whether it's choosing to attack those Trogs or deciding how much cream to put in your coffee. So don't be an ass." She smiles sugar all over the medicine she just fed him.

Brice hushes right up.

I ask, "How certain, then?"

"Mostly," answers Phil. "More than that. Dylan, we grew up with Grays. I know how they think, at least as much as any human can. I think I understand this thing they have with the Trogs. I believe if we capture those Grays, we'll win control."

"Are you willing to bet your life on it?"

"If you choose to believe me," says Phil, "that's exactly what I'm doing, right? We're all in this together."

I give the information a minute to sink in. I look around at the faces of my bridge crew, of my commandos who've been happy to sit silently and spectate. I need to make my choice first. "Those Grays are holed up in a rec room down on sub seven. Does your plan include a way to reach them?"

Phil grins. "It does."

Chapter 47

We're strapped into the platoon compartment—me, Brice, Silva, Lenox, and Mostyn—my commando team. Our magazines are full, topped off from the supplies we had the foresight to pilfer from Juji Station before we left earth's orbit. I'm carrying four grenades and three C4 charges. Each of us is.

Jill's mining tug is moving into position to support our assault. Her people know the situation. They know their part in the plan. We're all clear on the objective.

Penny is on the bridge, pushing the ship to a speed Phil guesses will make this whole thing work just right. Jablonsky is on the radio, coordinating with Blair and making sure everything happens by the deadline.

The inertial bubble is glowing blue around us. I can sense the grav field pulse strong in the Rusty Turd's aft drive array. In a few short minutes, Phil will power up the grav lens, and the main cabin will blaze bright.

"Major Kane," Jablonsky calls to me.

"Yes?"

"Colonel Blair wants to postpone."

My God, that woman is going to be the source of all my future stress-induced diseases. "Why?"

"She doesn't have confidence."

"In?"

"All of it."

"Radio her back," I tell Jablonsky, "and tell her I need some hard specifics and I need them now because we're on our attack run and we're not deviating without something more solid then watery bowels."

A moment passes.

Brice elbows me. "What?"

I roll my eyes. "Fucking Blair."

He nods. I've explained enough. Looking at the glowing blue waves crawling over the walls he asks, "We still going in?"

I nod.

"Good."

Jablonsky is back on the comm. "She doesn't believe we'll impact in the right place. She doesn't think we can break through."

Exasperating. Still, I have time before we ram our target. "Does she know Phil has super-genius grav sense? He's been out here in the ship scanning the Potato's interior for two solid days. It's like he's been taking an MRI of the colony's interior structures. He knows that rock better than she knows her face in the mirror. He knows the point on the surface we need to ram. He knows the angle we need to hit to end up where we want to be. Tell her that. Tell her quick."

I wait.

Thirty seconds pass.

Jablonsky informs me, "She wants Tarlow to consult. He knows the geology of these asteroids. He understands the size of the force it will take to shatter them."

"Valid point." Mostly. "Phil can see interior structures in the rock Tarlow can only guess at. It's a toss-up."

Jablonsky passes that message along, and comes back with, "She can't accept that Penny can drive the ship through a hundred and fifty feet of rock to get down to level seven, and even if she could, the energy of the collision would probably kill everybody on the Potato."

Dammit!

I'm done. "Tell her she should have listened more carefully when we brought her into the plan. We're ramming the asteroid from the side. We only have to break through eleven feet of stone to bust into the main corridor running across sub seven. Lastly, tell her it's too late to back out. Phil is already burning the g's. The Grays inside the Potato see us coming. Right now they're surprised and trying to figure out what we're up to. If we back out, we'll never have surprise on our side again." I look at the time on my d-pad. "Impact in thirty seconds. Tell her to prepare her people."

I comm the bridge crew. "Are we on track?"

"Impact in twenty-five seconds," Penny assures me.

I pass it along to my squad, and brace in my seat.

Phil powers up the grav lens. The bug in my head protests to the intense field forming up behind my seat.

If the Grays didn't see us coming before, they do now.

"Ten seconds!" shouts Penny.

Everyone is tense.

I take one more breath.

The cabin bursts in a flash of blinding blue. The ship shudders. My head swims.

Sound!

I hear wind rushing as the blue light fizzles away.

"In!" Penny shouts. "We're in!"

"On target!" Phil confirms. "Through sub seven, through three—no four—rooms."

I pop my seat harness free, jump to my feet, and comm the squad, "Time to pay the rent!"

Chapter 48

The outer wall of the main corridor on sub seven is broken open to space, and all the air in the station is flowing through vertical passageways and horizontal halls and decompressing out into the void. Airlock doors on every room are closing automatically. Alarms are blaring over the blast of the wind.

Having broken through eleven feet of outer shell as well as the thick stone walls separating four more rooms before coming to a stop, the ship is lying in a torrential eddy as the station's atmosphere rushes past the holes behind us. Its backwash is howling like a deep-throated ghost, enormous and wicked.

"Careful," Phil calls over the comm.

"Are you coded into the local network?" I ask, as I jump through an assault door down to a cracked floor just a few feet below me. My auto grav pulls my feet down and holds me in place against the buffeting wind.

"We're logged on to the network," Jablonsky tells me.

I'm glad it still functions.

"That wall to your left," says Phil. "That's the one you want."

"How so?" asks Brice. The plan was to bust in and then rush down the hallway to attack the defending Trogs before they could recover from the impact of the collision and the tornado of decompressing gases.

"We're a lot farther inside than we planned to be," Phil rushes through the words. "There's a dorm on the other side of that wall. On the other side of the dorm is the rec room. Blow two walls, and you've found the Grays without having to go through the hall and the bulk of the defending Trogs."

Assuming the decompression hasn't blown them all into space.

"You're a godsend," Brice tells him.

Aw, the kids are playing nice. I'm all teary-eyed. Not.

Brice is at the wall in two seconds placing a C4 charge, and I'm rushing everyone back into the ship, explaining as we go.

Once inside, I comm Phil, "Can you sense the Grays? Are they still in the rec room?"

"Yes." He's certain. "They're confused. Dazed is a better word. Being so close to a grav lens collision has left them stunned."

"The ghost Trogs?" I ask. I know there are six in there with the Grays.

"Everyone is down. The only Trogs on this level who are moving are the ones in the hall being blown out into space."

Brice jumps in through the open assault door, glancing hurriedly at me. "Ready?"

"Everybody brace." I give Brice a nod.

I hear the explosion and feel the blast through the ship. The wind changes as the dorm decompresses.

"Wait a few seconds," I tell my squad as they rush for the opening.

Brice is in the assault door, nodding his head with each silent beat he counts. Outside the ship, every manner of furniture, whole and shattered, is furiously blowing past.

As soon as it settles to the floor, Brice is out again.

"Go!" I shout at my team.

We're all out in a flash.

I point to the wall Brice just blasted a hole in. "Here, line up here. Backs to the wall. Remember your assignment."

Brice is already through the hole, running to the next wall, and placing a charge. That's the wall between the dorm and the main rec room.

Silva, Lenox, Mostyn and me throw our backs against the already-breached wall and grav tight.

"As soon as the decompression wave settles," I tell them. "Rush in. Kill the Trogs. Capture the Grays."

"Placing the charge," Brice tells us, panting from the sprint. "You can feel the grav all the way in here." He's talking about the rec room gravity. According to Tarlow, it's the only room in the station with full-time, simulated earth g.

We wait.

Seconds pass. They feel like minutes.

Brice pops out through the breach and takes his spot against the wall beside me. "Ready?"

It's a warning, not a question. He pushes the big red dot.

The explosion rocks us again.

Pieces of rock come through the breach first, followed by pool furniture and truckloads of water from the pool, turning into mist as it converts from liquid to gas in near-zero pressure. All of it washes past us, spreading into our room, flowing over the Rusty Turd, and blasting out through the fractured walls behind.

A ghost Trog sails past us, unconscious, and smashes against the bow of our ship. Lenox fires a dozen rounds into him before his body is carried by the wind into the next room.

The howl settles down.

Decompression complete.

I jump through the breach, Brice on my heels, racing across the chaotic dorm, toward the hole in the far wall. Silva and Lenox start the search of the jumbled dorm. Mostyn stands in the breach, defensive grav set at the max, making sure no Gray escapes past her. Everybody following the plan.

CHAPTER 49

"Ghost down," calls Silva. She's the first to score a kill, not counting the Trog who flew out with the decompressing air and pool water.

"Gray!" shouts Lenox. "Two! I have them."

The rec room is impossibly huge with an empty swimming pool taking up nearly half the floor space and sport courts taking up the rest. The light glowing down from above looks like sunlight. The gravity feels like home. It seems impossible, given that it's been burrowed from the heart of an asteroid a billion miles from earth.

I'm scanning the pool area doing the quick, simple math —four Grays and four ghost Trogs unaccounted for.

"The rest are in the rec room," Phil assures over the comm.

"Alive?" I ask.

"The Grays are," he answers.

Brice finds a ghost Trog on its hands and knees near a wall in a jumble of deck chairs. A long burst from his railgun kills it.

Three Trogs left. "Can you tell where the others are?" I ask Phil, as I run to the edge of the pool and see two Grays and a ghost Trog lying in the bottom near the drain. The Grays are moving like they're sick. The Trog is sitting up and raising his head to look at me. I jump into the pool, grabbing my disruptor off my back as I fly. I can't risk killing the Grays with deflected railgun slugs.

The Trog tenses at the last second as his senses clarify enough for him to understand what's happening. Too late, though. My disruptor splits his helmet. Into the comm, I announce, "Two Grays in the bottom of the pool." I kill my auto grav and go airborne, shooting up near the thirty-foot ceiling.

Railgun rounds spray across the width of the rec room, coming from the hole we just blew in the wall, all the way to the far corner. It's Silva shooting.

She's peppering an ebony Trog who's raising his railgun as Silva's rounds deflect in every direction. Brice fires diagonally across the room, and I add my gun to the onslaught. The Trog falls as the rounds penetrate and then shred him in a puff of red and gore.

I'm scanning.

"Another Gray," calls Brice, pulling one by the foot out from beneath a large upturned shelf.

"The last one is heading for the door!" shouts Phil.

God, I envy his grav sense.

I turn toward the main door and spot the Gray, immediately pouring on the g to accelerate after him and catch him before he pogos his way through.

A blur materializes from my right.

"Trog!" shouts Silva, and the air lights up with red railgun rounds.

I dive for the floor, just to change my course, and the Trog zips past above me.

Silva's rounds follow it.

"I got it," Brice shouts. "You get that Gray."

I trust them and max grav to close the gap, grabbing the Gray by his neck as his hand grasps the doorknob.

Spinning around with a one-handed grip on my railgun I bring it to bear on the last Trog, but see him hitting the far wall and falling limply toward the floor.

"That's it for the Trogs," I tell them, dropping my gun to dangle on its harness. I spin and go to work placing a C4 charge on the door, look at the Gray in my hand and smile. "You're going to tell those fuckers in the hall aren't you?" I laugh, knowing I don't have to booby trap them. They know they can't come through without dying. It's better than a booby trap.

I laugh. It probably doesn't matter, at least not for a little bit. Any Trogs who were out there have to be flailing in the void right now.

"Grab 'em up," says Brice. "Let's go."

We have all six Grays.

Now for the hard part. Or easy part. I can only guess which. As far as I know, nothing like this has ever been tried before.

CHAPTER 50

We've consolidated our position.

The Grays are all sitting at the bottom of the empty pool. I'm standing in front of them with Phil at my side. Brice and Silva are behind them, guns unnecessarily ready.

Jill is perched on the edge of the pool with Lenox and Mostyn beside her. Jill's platoon is securing sublevel seven. They didn't have to fight for it, all of the Trogs in the hall, the lobby, or in front of the rec room were blown out into space when the station decompressed.

The asteroid is still crawling with Trogs, and they'll be coming to rescue their masters.

Blair is clucking away on the comm, although I've tuned her out, instead instructing Jablonsky to listen in and warn me if the Trogs attack that level.

"Phil," I ask, looking at the six Grays. "Which one is in charge?"

Phil points to the second one from the end, the one I caught trying to escape through the door.

"Can you communicate with it?"

Phil nods.

"Are you communicating with it now?"

Phil nods again.

"Tell it we want the Trogs to surrender."

"I did," Phil tells me. "It's arguing with me."

"How so?"

Phil turns to me. "You know. Hairy monkey this, ignorant beast that. Insulting things. It doesn't recognize us as worthy of having a conversation with."

"So it won't tell its Trogs to surrender."

Phil shakes his head. "It's confident in the next hour or so, we'll all be dead. It keeps telling me to leave it alone so it can rest and I can prepare to die with dignity."

"Uh, huh." I need to make a decision, and as is not uncommon, I have too many variables and too many choices.

I step over to the Grays and tap the leader on the head with my knuckles. It glares at me and shakes its head to knock my hand away. "This one?" I ask. "This one is the leader?"

"Yes," Phil answers.

I nod as I think through what I want to do. Maybe it'll work. Maybe not. What do I have to lose by trying? My humanity? I don't think so. Grays aren't humans. Like Trogs, they're monsters. It should be easy to do what I have in mind.

I reach down, snap the Gray up by his neck, and throw him. He flies three meters and hits the wall of the pool.

Phil grunts like he's been punched.

Others gasp.

Nobody expected that.

The Gray is on the floor of the pool, rolling over and picking himself up. I pounce on him, kicking him in the head and sending his spindly body spinning again. I have to jump over to where he lands and catch him. He's moving all jerky and quick, quick for a Gray. He's afraid. I can feel the emotion flowing out of him as palpable as Gray stink back in my house.

Phil is babbling something, but he doesn't understand what I need to do. He's too humane in his heart, that's why I didn't consult him before I started.

I grab one of the Gray's spindly arms, lift him and carry him until I'm standing a pace in front of the other five. I throw him to the ground and smash my boot onto his leg, and increase the downward grav in my suit while I twist and grind. The leg starts to come apart beneath my foot. I feel the pulpy tissue separate and ooze.

Phil's crying out. He's horrified. I turn down his comm so I won't have to listen at full volume.

When I lift my foot, the Gray twig is flattened, mush.

It's terrified. I can feel it, though at the same time, can't comprehend it.

"It's asking you to stop," Phil shouts, his voice cracking with distress.

I know, or hope he's not empathizing too much with the little beast, and I know the Gray is forcing Phil to share its suffering. It's like a broadcast, and I'm only getting part of the signal.

Stomping on the Gray's undamaged leg, I ask, "Is it begging?"

"What?" Phil's mortified.

I grind and the thing's agony creeps through me almost like I'm feeling it myself, so I fight it with my rage. I won't allow this grotesque little monster to rule my thoughts, and with that, I make my final choice. I stomp its skull.

My head pounds with sudden migraine force.

I stomp again, and it feels like I'm bashing my skull.

I stomp and kick, feeling all of it, going dizzy with pain, until the Gray's head splits open. I smash it one more time to open it up, and I stagger back from the intensity of searing agony, tearing my brain.

Gasping, I catch my balance, and go back for more.

The Gray's body is twitching, the orange symbiont is squirming, trying to burrow deeper inside the tick's split skull. I see its skin bubbling and peeling. It can't take the harsh vacuum like its Gray host can.

Dropping to a knee, I reach into the open skull, grab the orange mass and pull it out.

Pain fries my every nerve as I rip the last shred of its connection to the Gray body and throw it down on the pool floor. With nothing but blinding torment and aching rage, I go to work again with my boot, grinding the symbiont into goop.

The Gray's body goes still.

My agony disappears like it was never there.

I can breathe again.

Suddenly, I'm aware of everything around me, the universe isn't just me and orange torment. Five Grays are still lying on the floor, waving their arms like they're sick. Silva is down on her back. Phil is on his hands and knees bawling. Lenox, Mostyn, and Jill are off their feet.

They all felt it, at least some of it.

Only Brice is still standing, and I can see from the look on his face he's experienced his share of what that Gray just did to us. He stood hard through it, ready to back me up.

"Phil." I walk over to him and help him to his feet.

All of the others are moving, trying to regain their wits. I know they're alive, I know the suffering was imaginary. They have to be okay.

"Phil." I put an arm around him and hug him tight, probably the first time we've had contact that intimate and sincere since his brother died all those years ago. No, twice now in as many hours. Our relationship is changing. "Phil, I'm sorry about that. It had to be done." I rap the side of his helmet with my knuckles. "Phil, do you hear me?"

He nods. His blubbering is subsiding. "That was the most horrible thing I've ever felt."

"Yeah." I'm already making a new rule for dealing with Grays—don't make them suffer. Kill them quickly, or they'll fuck you.

With the memory of all that hurt suddenly refreshed, I'm suddenly inspired to find some retribution.

I leap away from Phil, draw my disruptor off my back and as the blade comes alive in blue, I swing it through the heads of two Grays. Their skulls come apart, sending orange symbiont goo in a spray across the pool.

The pain is sharp and quick, like a jab from a needle poking a thousand times, all at once, all over your skin.

It goes as quickly as it comes.

I draw a deep breath. "Phil, talk to those other Grays. Ask them if they're ready to surrender."

"I—"

"Phil," I remind him. "Lots of lives depend on this. *Ask them.*"

Phil sniffles up as many tears as he can, and concentrates on the Grays.

"Can they understand you?" I ask.

He nods.

"Are you telling them?"

He nods again.

I walk over among them and start looking for the next one I'll have to convince. "Which one is in charge now."

"No!" Phil shouts, "You can't."

"I can!" God, I hope I can. "Which one?"

Others on the comm agree with Phil. The assault is on all of us.

"Wait," he pleads. "Wait."

I reach down and pick one up by the neck.

"Stop, stop," Phil tells me. "Stop. They can't choose that fast."

I hold the Gray out at shoulder level where I can look into his eyes and he can see my face. I give them some time to vote telepathically or whatever they do.

Phil closes his eyes and stands for a moment, motionless except for his breathing.

I look around at the others. Silva is on her feet, hate in her eyes. She has her weapon up, ready to kill the Grays now that she knows what they can do. Jill is looking down on us with a face I can't read. Lenox is holding Mostyn in her arms.

I turn back to Phil. "Well?"

"They surrender."

"And the Trogs?"

"They can't surrender," says Phil. "They're property. They do what they're told."

"And what's that?"

"Whatever you want."

Victory!

"Tell them all to go to the surface. They need to pile their weapons on the ground in front of the warehouse where they held the prisoners, then they all have to hike down to the bottom of the mine pit and sit in rows. If they do it fast enough, I won't kill any more of these Grays. Be sure everybody understands that last part."

Chapter 51

"Congratulations." Blair sounds like she has a cocklebur stuck in her throat.

Tarlow is bubbling with gratitude. "You saved us."

"It wasn't me." I look around at Phil, Brice, Silva, Jill, Lenox, and Mostyn. Penny and Jablonsky are close by, and so is the rest of Jill's platoon. "We did it together." We truly did. I start spinning up a pontification on leadership and teamwork to share, and I'm trying to come up with a clever opening line.

"The Trogs are doing what you told them," bubbles Tarlow. "The ones on the surface have already laid down their arms and are running toward the mine. All of them are doing exactly what you told them."

Blair finds her voice. "We own this base again. We've fulfilled our mission and we all did this together."

"Yes, ma'am." It's the best response for the moment. "Yes, we did." And there is plenty of truth in that, too.

"Before you get all full of yourself," Blair sounds satisfied, like maybe she's turned the tide of the game I keep hoping we've matured past playing, "you need to know that when the dust thinned, we were able to send a distress call."

Tarlow interrupts without apology, seeming eager to please me. "The connection between the control room and the radio dish array was damaged in the original attack a few months ago. It took me awhile, circumstances and all. I finished fixing it right before your ships arrived."

Not sure if I'm supposed to say something, I go with the generic. "Good work."

"Eight assault ships are on their way here," says Blair. "We would have been fine without you half-destroying the base."

"No doubt." I'm bored with this conversation. I drag my boot across the bottom of the pool, trying to rub the orange brain goo out of the tread.

"They'll be here in a few days," Blair assures me. "We would have held out that long on level three."

Why does she feel like this is important? I make a guess. "You did a good job, Blair. I'm proud of you."

"I don't need you to patronize me, Major."

Oops. Wrong guess.

I don't rise to it, though. In fact, I try not to laugh. With the artificial pain the murdered Grays hotwired into my nervous system rapidly turning into a repressed memory, I want to revel in thrill of victory. It's time to talk about something productive. "I'm sure we can squeeze a lot more info out of these Grays down here."

"With torture?" spits Blair.

With fuck you! But I don't say that. "If we can find the location of a Trog base or two, we'll have enough assault ships to do some damage. No, more than that. We've proven the effectiveness of these weapons. We can win this war. We can clear the Trogs out of the solar system. Are those eight all we have? Is that the whole Free Army fleet?"

"We have more."

"A lot more?" I push. "Some more? Isn't it about time we embrace one another in a circle of trust." I nearly laugh at that, too, because I think it's funny.

"I'm afraid you've pushed yourself right out of that circle, Major."

I exaggerate a sigh. Blair can't get past the games. "Look, you can stay here and be Queen of the Potato if you want. I'm going to steal Tarlow from you and maybe some of his buddies from downstairs and have them fix my ship. Then I'm going out with our little fleet to attack the Trogs. With any luck, you'll never have to see me again. So can we play nice until then? A few days, please?"

"Do you know a Lieutenant Holt?"

That stops me cold. When I recover, I say, "He was the platoon commander on my assault ship. We decided not to kill him. We put him off on Juji Station before we came here."

Blair laughs. Maybe cackle is a better word. And better than that, maybe chortle like a witch watching her favorite newt drown in a boiling cauldron.

I decide I really, really despise her, but I need to know what has her so tickled. "What?"

"The MSS is broadcasting a news vid where—"

"Propaganda vid," I correct.

"—Lieutenant Holt presents evidence that you're a Trog mole and you're responsible for the Arizona Massacre."

"The Arizona Massacre?" It has a name? That angers me. I can't believe it. "They're pinning that fiasco on me?"

"They claim you've been in league with the Trogs for years. You're the reason we're losing this war."

"Everybody knows the MSS is full of shit." Dismissiveness. I tell myself, that's the best play here. No point in getting wrapped up in MSS lies, even if they are personal.

"Nobody in the fleet will trust you," says Blair. "It doesn't matter what you've done. Nobody will believe those stories either. They'll assume all of your *heroic exploits* are lies."

"All bullshit. Total crap." This all goes back to that argument she and I had in front of the warehouse after I freed her. This is a power play. I know she's behind it, somehow. "We're all out here because we know what the MSS is. These soldiers will fight beside me. I'm not worried."

Blair isn't done. "What about Holt?"

"What about him?"

"He's SDF, maybe MSS. You were supposed to kill him, and you didn't. Even if everyone out here decides the MSS story is made up of lies, then what are they to think of Holt? Are you an SDF sympathizer? Are you going to betray us to them? Are these heroics your ruse to put all of our necks in a noose?"

"Fuck you." I close the connection. I'm steamed. I stomp around inside the pool, thinking about killing something else, maybe a Gray, maybe a Trog. I stop myself. It's Blair who deserves my anger.

God, I despise that woman.

Everyone around me is asking questions. None of them were on the comm with Blair and me. They don't know what's transpired.

I push through the effort to calm myself, and decide I'm not going to listen to Blair's shit. I'm going to do what I do.

I open a comm to my soldiers. "We've won. The asteroid is ours. The Trogs have surrendered. They're all marching toward the mine. Let's secure these prisoners. The Free Army fleet is coming. It's time to prepare the Rusty Turd for the battle with the Trogs' armada."

THE BATTLE CONTINUES…

A message from Colonel Blair...

(Okay, maybe a request for reviews wrapped in a fun story?)

Please, allow me to introduce myself. I'm Beverly Blair, but you know me as Colonel Blair, perhaps derogatorily as 'Queen of the Potato.'

I just want to say, I greatly resent that one, and want to express in no uncertain terms that Dylan Kane is an immature dunce. He's got a third-grade boy's cruel heart and I can assure you, he'll lead this whole endeavor to ruin.

So please, pay attention when I tell you, don't encourage him by reading this terrible compilation of half-truths and self-indulgent absurdities. I'm a good person and he makes me look like a total bitch. In truth, I think he has mommy issues. In fact, I'm certain of it. I could tell you some things. I know one he didn't tell you—among other things, he's afraid of flying monkeys.

I know!

Flying monkeys. Can you believe it?

Who the hell's afraid of flying monkeys? And that's just the first on a long list. He's a total sissy.

The point I'm trying to get to is this. We don't want Dylan Kane to torture us with any more of this sophomoric swill, am I right? So let's all agree, whatever we do, we won't buy the next book in the series:

http://smarturl.it/Amz-FreedomFray

And we won't check out this link for the free prequel and email list signup:

http://smarturl.it/FreedomsSiege-Free

We absolutely won't go back to the place we purchased the book and leave a review. I mean, really, do I even have to tell you this?

http://smarturl.it/Amz-FreedomFury

And of course, we won't **Like** Bobby Adair, Author on Facebook.

Let's be honest, if Dylan Kane had a shred of self-respect he wouldn't need the ephemeral adulation of social-media-centric cyber relationships. Kane should buy a goldfish. They make good pets and are like training wheels for the immature men in our lives who need a dependable starter relationship.

Thank you for your time,

Colonel Beverly Blair

Ministry of State Security

Reviews are awesome and a great way to bank some good Karma. Please visit the site where you purchased the book to leave a quick review, or just some stars if you liked it...many thanks!

And to learn more about Kane's dad, sign up for our we-hate-spam-too mailing list, and get Freedom's Siege, the free prequel to Freedom's Fire: http://smarturl.it/FreedomsSiege-Free

MORE ABOUT BOBBY'S OTHER BOOKS...

Slow Burn Series (9 books), a best-seller!

Slow Burn is Bobby's flagship post-apocalyptic zombie series, but so much more than a zombie book. Follow the adventures of Zed as he wakes up one morning to find that something's a little different in the world. As the world is going to shit, Zed meets up with Murphy, and they try to navigate their new reality through a world of the "slow burns" before they are completely consumed by the virus. Great reviews, with over a million books sold, readers LOVE this one.

The Last Survivors Series (6 books)

A collaborative series with fellow zombie author T.W. Piperbrook, this series has a little more of a Sci-Fi feel, popular with folks who like Game of Thrones. It explores what happens 300 years in the future after the apocalypse, when man has rebuilt and gone back to an almost medieval society.

Ebola K: A Terrorism Thriller (trilogy)

A really great terrorism thriller with awesome reviews. It focuses on the devastating Ebola outbreak and the possibility of weaponized Ebola by terrorist organizations and nationalized resources like blood with Ebola antibodies. A more in-depth and complex observation of the real world. This series follows an American college student teaching in Uganda as the country comes under attack from the deadly virus as he tries to make his way back to the safety of his family back in the United States.

It's also historically and medically accurate, so you'll learn a little about the history of the disease as well.

Black Rust, Black Virus (first two in a series)

A newer series from Bobby that also deals with a different post-apocalyptic reality. Christian Black is a bounty hunter charged with hunting down the infected…a "Regulator." When caught in an unsanctioned kill, Christian sets about to clear his name. A fairly deep character, whose flaws are an important backstory to his adventurous life.

Dusty's Diary: One Frustrated Man's Zombie Apocalypse Story (first in a series)

Fun and crass…be careful if you're easily offended! Has some great advice about what to pack in your post-apocalyptic bunker (don't forget the porn!). Dusty's Diary has an uncertain future…people like it, so I'll probably write more in the future. This is a short story.

Made in the USA
Columbia, SC
04 September 2021